GOLDEN HARVEST

To The Andersen Family,
I hope you are blessed by
this story!

GOLDEN HARVEST

ROSANNA C. SHARPS

Word Sower Publishing

Copyright © 2010 by Rosanna C. Sharps

All rights reserved. This book or any portion thereof may not be reproduced or used in any manner whatsoever without the express written permission of the publisher except for the use of brief quotations in a book review.

"Exploration and Settlement: 1820-1835" map courtesy of the University Libraries, The University of Texas at Austin.

Book cover and interior design by Michael Sharps.

Cover photo and Snelling photos by Michael Sharps.
www.sharpsphotography.com

Printed in the United States of America

First Printing, 2011

Library of Congress Control Number: 2011929201

ISBN: Softcover   978-0-9834474-0-5
          Hardcover   978-0-9834474-1-2
          eBook   978-0-9834474-2-9

Word Sower Publishing
www.WordSowerPublishing.com

I would like to extend my gratitude to
those who assisted in my efforts in
publishing "Golden Harvest."

To God, for His inspiration.
To my husband, Michael, for his support.
To Shirley, for her encouragement.
To Margaret, for providing historical resources for Snelling.

PREFACE

Jonathan and Mary Sawyer have both been given direction from God to move their family from the war torn town of Perryville, Kentucky in 1864 to their new land of promise... Snelling, California. But the land of promise is not without its 'giant' encounters for the family, especially for their children who are coming of age. It came in the form of disappointing ambitions, uncontrollable temptations, hidden intentions, bad discernment and a desire to follow a calling. Jonathan and Mary discover their life assimilating the Parable of the Sower. The era occurs in the late 1800's, yet the trials are as timeless as the Parable itself. Although the family is fictitious, their life situations are not and the reader will find themselves relating to the struggles and the victories the family encounters. In addition to the main characters are actual people, places and situations that occurred in California's frontier towns such as Jamestown, Chinese Camp, Coulterville, Mariposa, Rio Vista and of course Snelling. The names of the actual people have been slightly changed and the story is based upon historical fact. This story will open the eyes of the reader to the difficulties that can easily occur in life and how faith in an almighty and all-knowing God will take these difficulties and produce a golden harvest.

CONTENTS

1

Divine Direction

SPRING FINALLY ARRIVED in April of 1864, and the wagons were ready and packed for the six month journey ahead. The Sawyer family had only one more day left on their farm in Perryville, Kentucky, before moving out to California. Most people were hoping that the war would end at any time. The Sawyers did their best to stop the battle, at least in their minds, so that they could move forward in their lives, but their ravaged farm did not permit it.

The family was inside finishing their last minute packing while Jonathan silently sat on the front porch swing trying to reflect upon the good memories spent on the farm. Tears rolled down his cheek as he began thinking about these boyhood recollections growing up in his father's farmhouse bequeathed to him. He never dreamt that he would ever have to sell his inheritance and leave Perryville.

His thoughts moved immediately to the gut wrenching memories of the Civil War, and its affects on his family, and on the property. A year had gone by, and Jonathan was almost fully recovered from a Confederate gun shot wound to his right upper chest received while fighting in the Battle of Perryville, Kentucky, also known as the Battle of Chaplin Hills, on October 8, 1862.

The events of this horrifying time were still fresh in his mind, and it certainly left its scars upon himself, his loved ones and everywhere else he looked around in his little town of Perryville. Even his own property had been ravaged from that bloody battle.

Before the war began, Jonathan's father died and left his estate to him and his wife Mary, and children; Samuel who is now age fifteen, Sarah thirteen, Naomi nine, and David eight years old. Most of his wheat crops had been destroyed from the trampling of soldiers, animals, and fire. The livestock, excepting the poultry, was spared in agreement to offer his farmhouse as a temporary military hospital.

Strewn throughout their home and barn were the wounded men that Mary and the children were forced to tend. To this day, the family has nightmares of dying soldiers in blood drenched uniforms, some with missing limbs, and others whose bodies appeared to be torn inside out. The cries of agony could still be heard, and everywhere they turned in their house, flashbacks would disturb their minds. Their home had become a memorial for the dead and Jonathan knew he had to get them as far from this place as he could.

The Sawyers lost almost everything due to the looting of the war. But Jonathan's father did leave a considerable amount of monetary inheritance, in addition to the property, for he and his sister, Noelle, who had moved North with her husband and children. At the age of thirteen, he lost his mother to the pox.

In October of 1863, after Jonathan's one year anniversary of being shot, God put a heavy burden upon Jonathan's heart to move them from their devastated home and town. The next few days were spent in prayer looking for direction from the Lord. Then, on the following Sunday, they attended church and the Pastor began his message from Genesis 12:1, *"Now the LORD had said to Abram: Get out of your country, from your family and from your father's house, to a land that I will show you…"*

Upon hearing this, Jonathan remembered how he and his wife both looked at each other with awe because they believed God gave them the direction they had prayed for. The Promised Land, California, is the destination they felt God was sending them. There they can purchase property in a state which had not been touched by the affects of the war, and where wheat farming was desired.

So the farm was put up for sale on November 1863, and it sold in March of 1864. The hopeful couple packed two of their covered wagons with supplies necessary for their entire family for the six-month journey across the vast, Great Plains of North America to California, a distance of approximately 2,400 miles.

Thirty-eight year old Jonathan has a dark brown shaggy mane of hair which began to recede along the top corners of his forehead. Farming helped him to develop strong arms, back, and hands, and a lean but muscular build to his five feet eight inches tall stature.

Also in her late thirties, Mary has thick wavy long brown tresses which she wore parted down the middle. The braids of her hair on the left and right side and in the back of her head, are wrapped together to form a taut bun. Bound in a working corset and simple day dress is her slender but sturdy five feet four inches tall frame. Although she worked hard on the farm and is a mother of four offspring; her soft, pale complexion still shone smooth and radiant, and her hazel colored eyes are kind and compassionate. Her husband and children adored her warm and tender smile and her loving touch.

The eldest son, Samuel, was almost as tall and handsome as his father. Like his mother, his thick shortly cropped wavy brown hair was cut above his ears, and flowed a little longer on the top and back. To move westward to where the sun sets is what his adventurous, strong spirit longed for.

The youngest of the siblings is David whose gentle ole soul lives in his eight year old body. His wavy russet mane flowed in layers about his head. Any mother's heart would melt for a son with big brown puppy dog eyes and a sweet disposition. Yet he had the wisdom and cautious discernment of all three older siblings put together possibly because he is the baby of the family, and is always well protected, and overshadowed.

The eldest of the daughters, Sarah, stands five feet three inches tall with lengthy auburn curls. It parted down the middle and is pulled to the back of her head, where over a dozen soft ringlets are bound neatly with a ribbon. Like Mary, Sarah too, has a supple and pale complexion, plus a small dimple to the right of her lips, which added a pinch of charm when she smiled.

The younger of the two sisters, Naomi, currently stood at five feet tall but is growing. Similar to her father are her long straight bronze tresses that she wore like her mothers, braided on three sides, and formed together in a bun. Known as the rambunctious child, her stocky frame suited farming more than her sister's ladylike figure. Considered a handsome young lady her facial features showed hints of her father's appearance. Compared to David, she was clever, but not always wise, and she found herself to be pushing the boundaries her parents set for her.

As a form of comfort and relaxation to get their minds off the war, the Sawyers enjoyed playing music. The instrument Jonathan played is the banjo, Samuel the fiddle, Sarah the mandolin, Naomi the dulcimer, David the spoons and Mary clogged to the wonderful old-time tunes they performed. The joyous melodies will make their long, dusty journey more pleasant and enjoyable for everyone.

The back half of the wagons had their carefully packed belongings. To the front and behind the driver's wood bench seat, is the bedding or sitting area where passengers can relax or sleep during the drive.

The family's clothing was neatly arranged in layers into the large, heavy cedar chest which Mary's mother passed down to her after her death. Traveling as light as they could, they each brought two sets of apparel. The boys would bring wool and linen pants, cotton shirts, vests, frock coats and overcoats, and slouch hats. The girls selected two prairie and day dresses, aprons, petticoats, undergarments, straw hats, and bonnets.

Also, placed in the chest are Mary's books, which she collected as a child.

The plan Jonathan had was to grow wheat in California, so he packed sacks of seed along with the smaller, but necessary, tools for farming and maintaining the wagons.

Food consisted of lightweight, non-perishables like dried

fruits and vegetables, flour, corn meal, beans, jerky, bacon, sugar, coffee, tea, salt, spices, and condiments. Three hens and a rooster were brought along for fresh eggs and the men would hunt for game as they traveled on the trail. Cookware consisted of a cast iron pot, a skillet, a coffee percolator, a gallon kettle, and several cooking utensils. Six, ten gallon water barrels, are to be filled and emptied on steep climbs to lighten the load.

The two wagons consisted of four oxen each. The first would tow a cow and a horse. The other towed another horse and one more ox. The wagon train aimed to travel an average of fifteen miles per day. Jonathan and Mary planned to drive the wagons, with Samuel and Sarah taking the reins through the less difficult passages. The four would take turns riding the horses when needed, to move the strong, but slow-moving oxen. The boys, including the family hound dogs Boomer and Ann, are to ride with Mary, and the girls with Jonathan.

WHILE JONATHAN WAS REFLECTING on the events leading up to their trip to California, Mary sat down next to him on the swing. Noticing his tear swollen eyes, she wrapped her arms around his and laid her head upon his shoulder.

"I know how difficult this is fer ya, Jonathan. It is fer me too. But I am so excited to see what God has in store fer us in California," said Mary being positive.

"Oh Mary, as much as I love this place, I cain't seem to get these bad memories out of my mind. The good times we've had here have been overshadowed by the war," explained Jonathan, trying to hold back his emotions. "I do look forward to our fresh, new start in this land of promise." Jonathan reiterated God's direction, wiping the tears away from his eyes with his sleeves and tried to cheer up his disposition.

"Thank the Lord fer the many pioneers who already paved the way to this territory of golden harvests and vast opportunities, Mary, so we shouldn't be afraid 'bout movin' West. It'll be a place of new beginnings fer us an' the family."

After he described the journey, Jonathan remarked as he watched the sun setting from the front porch, "Think of it Mary! Just beyond that horizon is where the land finally ends its boundaries and the ocean frames its shores!"

California is characteristic of the Promised Land flowing with milk and honey for many people. But the milk and honey is more like gold and productive property to purchase. This is what Jonathan and Mary prayed for and desired for their family now that the war was coming to an end. They needed a fresh start in undamaged territory.

"Well, we're gonna need plenty of strength fer tomorra'. Supper is ready. Let's sit down with the children and ask God's blessin'," Mary insisted. "Then we better get ta bed, so we can have enough rest an' wake early."

In the kitchen, they joined hands to have their last meal in the farmhouse while Jonathan said grace, "Heavenly Father, we appreciate yer kindness and mercy upon our family and the direction you have given us to follow after you to the land of promise. We thank ya for yer provision, Lord, and trust ya to guide and protect us as we travel west to California. Thank ya, Lord, for this food we are about to receive. In Jesus' name, we pray. Amen."

2

Westward Journey

PPARENTLY A NEW WAGON TRAIN congregated
every month to set off to California. In April 1864,
the Sawyers joined their wagons with fifty other
pioneering families journeying west to California.

After five months of grueling travel throughout the Great
Plains of North America, they finally arrived at Carson City,
Nevada, the town on the eastern side of the Sierra Mountain
Range of California. It was the wagon train captain's second
time to traverse on the California Trail and Central Overland
Route, so he was aware of the prime camping locations and the
precautionary measures needed in case of possible encounters
with either the Indians or outlaws that troubled this lawless
territory. They journeyed from Fort Laramie, Wyoming;
downward to Salt Lake City, Utah; then through the dry
wasteland called the Forty Mile Dessert.

The Sierra Mountain Range was the last hurdle to overcome
before finally arriving in the lush flatlands of California. But

before they tackled the steep 7100 foot ascent, the wagons had to be lightened tremendously. The water barrels are emptied, and heavy furnishing sold off. For Mary, this meant that she had to part with her mother's cedar hope chest and the many books she had collected as an adolescent. Both she and Jonathan had wrestled with this inevitable fact since the time they left Perryville. But now with the mountain range in view, she knew that she had lost the match. And so she reluctantly sold off her precious possessions in Carson City, with her husbands promise to repurchase these items in California, once they established themselves.

Carson City, Nevada, allowed the travelers three days of respite before starting into the steepest segment of their journey. Although fatigued, the family anxiously awaited to resume on the trail again so that they can complete their sojourn and call California their home.

"How much longer till we arrive, Pa?" Naomi grumbled while peering out of the wagon.

"Ya see them hills over yonder?" Jonathan replied pointing at the stretch of Sierra's in the distance. "First, we will need to get over them. Once we are on the other side, we'll go south a way, until we get to the valley floor and find some flat farm land. So, I figure maybe we have another month," Jonathan assured.

In early September, the mountain temperatures plummeted at night. Jonathan and Mary retained their stoves although they added a tremendous amount of weight to the wagons. The cold nights ahead had cause for more concern than hauling the heavy load up the steep grades, so they made sure the oxen stopped as often as necessary to rest.

THE LEANER WAGON train was once again prepared to move on for the last sector of the journey through the Sierra Mountain Range. The barrels no longer needed filling because of the abundance of water and grazing meadows throughout the Carson River trail.

"Come on, Fire!" Samuel jerked back on his horse's reins to lift his head up and away from consuming the tall grass along the trail. "Keep a movin'. There'll be plenty to eat, Boy, when we stop fer a break."

Yelling, Samuel rode his horse beside the oxen to motivate them to press forward. "Hee-yah, hee-yah!"

The first range of mountains to tackle is the Carson Range. To get there, they would have to traverse through the Carson River Valley. The wagons had to barrel over large boulders with ropes, pry bars, and levers, and also cross over several bridges. The wheels creaked as they maneuvered over the uneven and rocky ground. The items inside were tossed about, and the children did their best to keep things securely in place. Sarah and Samuel rode the horses as they crossed the river and led the extra oxen and cow. This was safer and easier this way for the animals.

After passing the valley, the Carson Mountain Range in the Sierras would be a 7,100 foot ascent before reaching the beautiful Hope Valley. A few years earlier, the Mormon Battalions had removed most of the largest boulders and widened the pass for the wagons. This made the Carson trail the preferred choice rather than traveling the Truckee and Donner Pass north of Lake Tahoe.

The trail would wind, twist, and turn up the mountainside as it progressed higher in elevation. Just when they thought they were at the top of the mountain, another level met them at the bend. Finally, they did reach the summit. Passing the Carson Range would take about five days with ample rest between grades.

Once in Hope Valley, the terrain leveled, although the altitude created some difficulty. The air was thinner and made breathing strenuous for a while until the lungs could acclimate.

The handy-work of God can be seen in this mountainous region. The fresh scent of pine permeated the atmosphere; and the bright yellow, red, and orange colors of the oak, maple, and aspen trees painted the landscape. The river flowed with soothing calm this time of the year because the snow had already melted leaving a lush green valley floor. Wild mountain flowers of lavender, crimson, and chartreuse covered the meadows. And the music of the stream splashing against the boulders would lull any tired soul to sleep.

Much of the wildlife simultaneously became a blessing and a curse. The deer, the fresh-water salmon, and trout served well for meals. The little, curious, furry critters such as the ground squirrels, raccoons, and possums often visited the camps.

The animals, which posed as the most dangerous to the camp, are the brown bears, mountain lions, wolves, and coyotes. The night watchmen had been doubled because of these wild creatures. On several occasions, bears were caught breaking into unattended wagons scavenging for food, and mountain lions were shot while attacking some of the sheep and chicken.

Trappers can be seen across the trail with loads of beaver fur, a hot item of trade in these days. But the greatest commodity in California is of course the gold discovered in 1849 which could be found while panning along the rivers. Travelers would often stop to pan next to the Carson River. The large veins of gold in the mountains were exposed north of Hope Valley in mines or in the American River which flowed near Placerville. This little town is the destination for the majority of the pioneers.

"Pa, what are those men doin' over there at the side of the river?" Samuel inquired as he noticed them squatting, seemingly washing dishes.

"I believe they are pannin' fer gold," Jonathan replied as he slowed the oxen to form a circle with the others.

"Ya mean like yer weddin' ring?" Samuel asked with curiosity, trying to figure out why they would search for jewelry in this remote area.

"Yep. But the gold is still in its natural state, similar to a small rock, a grain of sand, or even flakes of snow, all mixed up with the mud. Some collect the nuggets and exchange it fer money at the bank. Others sell it to jewelers to melt and fashion it into jewelry…yep, like my weddin' ring," Jonathan explained as they stopped to set up camp in Hope Valley. They would stay here for five days to allow the oxen to rest and recuperate from any abrasions which resulted from the friction of the harnesses during the steep climb.

"That sounds like fun. I betcha a feller can get rich that way!"

"I reckon. But I hear it is risky business. Ya better stick to farmin'. It is a lot more dependable." Jonathan justified himself as he unhitched the oxen.

The wagons were formed in a circle, as they have done each evening on the journey, with the livestock collected in the center, so they would not run off. After the men had watered them, they went out to the river to catch fish and hunt for wild game and the women began their evening meal preparation.

"Naomi and David! Please gather some wood or buffalo chips, so I can start a fire!" Mary called out.

"What cha cookin' tonight, Ma?" Sarah asked.

"It depends on Pa and Samuel, and how well they do at huntin' today." Mary balanced herself while shuffling through the wagon looking for her wooden cooking utensils and cast iron pot.

"Why don't ya help me by cuttin' up some taters' and carrots, Sarah?" handing the vegetables to her. "I'll start the fire."

The sound of pots and pans banging around could be heard throughout the camp as the women clamored through their wagons looking for their supplies and setting up their grills. The collected wood or buffalo chips are piled into a metal half barrel which stood above the ground on four legs.

Once the coals are hot and steady, a grill is placed on top of the half barrel. On one side of the grill, Mary did the cooking, while on the other, she boiled water in the gallon kettle for washing the dishes. A bucket of water is always kept nearby to extinguish the fire.

Several times, Jonathan, Samuel, Boomer, and Ann came back to camp with wild game in hand; sometimes pheasant, duck, jack rabbit, salmon, or trout. Large animals like deer, antelope, and buffalo are shared amongst the fifty families.

This day, Jonathan and Samuel, shot a couple of rabbits.

"Here ya are honey!" Jonathan said beaming with pride as

he plopped down the carcasses on a rickety wood table placed on top of wooden saw horse legs.

Skinned and cut up in pieces, Mary threw them in her cast iron pot with some seasoning and vegetables which Sarah chopped up. That night the family had a delicious rabbit stew for dinner.

This is the usual affair for the families every evening. The women would take the catch of the day, and pluck them or skin them, and fry them in the pan, or make a stew. The leftovers, if any, are kept for the next day's lunch along the way. Nothing went to waste on the trail.

The evening ended with a few rounds of old-time tunes, also known as hillbilly music, played by the Sawyer family. Songs filtered through the night air; *Oh Susanna*, *Beautiful Dreamer*, *Shall We Gather at the River*, and other melodies from the hills. The families stomped and clogged around their camp fires until they exhausted themselves and went to bed for an early rise. In the morning, the smell of freshly brewed coffee, biscuits, and bacon and eggs frying in the pan woke everyone from their deep sleep.

THE END OF THE TRAIL at Hope Valley is yet another 700 foot ascent called "the Devil's Ladder". Again, the pulleys and levers were used to get to the summit of the steep passes which hugged the edge of the mountain cliffs. The rope and pry bar marks left their scars on the tree trunks and rocks from all the previous travelers who combated this trail.

At the apex, they would travel along the Carson Pass on the Sierra Crest. Those whose destination is Placerville veered north, and the remaining continued on headed west towards Stockton.

As for the Sawyer family, they maintained the course until they reached a small town called Jackson. It took about three weeks from the time they left Carson City to arrive here. They rested and resupplied for two days in Jackson in preparation for the last week before arriving in Snelling.

"Yehaw!" Mary cried out as they began their descent from the Sierras. The mountainous landscape started changing from tall pines to wild oak trees. "We are finally past them hills! How much longer, John?"

"If all goes well, then maybe one more week!" Jonathan pulled on the reins as he yelled back. "Yer right, Mary. That mountain is sure pretty, but it near killed me tryin' to get these wagons up those steep climbs. The ole war wound was beginnin' to ache in my chest."

"Oh Lord! Are ya okay?" Mary pulled her wagon closer to Jonathan's concerned.

"I'm fine my love. Don't ya worry yer mind none," Jonathan tried to keep Mary from becoming anxious as he looked ahead and smiled ambiguously. He remembered how devastated she was when she almost lost him two years ago to the war.

FROM JACKSON, THEY HEADED SOUTH on what is called the Gold Country Highway which ran on the west side of the Sierra Mountain Range. It connected all the small mining towns such as Angel's Camp, Jamestown, China Camp, and Coulterville. This was about a seventy-five mile stretch, a seven-day journey.

On the second day along this highway, they arrived at Jamestown. This little town bustled with prospectors who rode in and headed straight for the bank where they had their gold findings weighed and traded for certificates equal the value.

Intrigued by them, Samuel found himself to be tagging along with one who had walked into town leading his equipment laden mule by the reins.

"Hey Mister, is there really gold in these mountains?" Samuel inquired with wide eyed curiosity.

"You betcha kid!" beamed the old prospector dressed in a worn out, mud stained pair of Levi jeans and muddied dark linen shirt. Stopping his mule he reached into a dusty leather pack hanging on its side and pulled out a small canvas sack. He untied it and poured its glimmering yellow contents into the palm of his hand. Six nuggets of gold lay shimmering in the sunlight.

"What does this look like to ya?" as he allowed Samuel to touch the shiny stones.

Samuel's jaw dropped as his finger tips braised over the precious treasure. "Whoa...I've never seen gold before. Thank ya fer showing this to me mister!" Watching him put them away, Samuel stood there dumbfounded. Little did Samuel know that it took him all summer to find those six nuggets.

"Sure son. Be careful now," the prospector wagged his index finger at Samuel. "Gold fever is very contagious!" Grabbing the reins of the mule, he turned and grinned displaying his coffee stained teeth, as he continued walking towards the bank.

"Sam! Don't ya get no ideas in that head of yers!" Mary cried out to Samuel who was standing in the center of the street mesmerized. "Son…help yer Pa water the animals!"

Samuel snapped out of his daze and looked over to Mary who stood by the wagon with her hands on her hips. "Huh… oh…all right, Ma, here I come!"

After completing his chores, they parked the wagons outside of town where they stayed the night.

The next day, they resumed on the Gold Country Highway until they arrived in Coulterville. From there, they veered towards the west on John Muir Highway for twelve miles. The immense valley floor could be seen from this vantage point. It was flat land, stretching almost the entire length of California, bordered by the Pacific Ocean on the horizon.

They continued south on Merced Falls Road for sixteen more miles, which brought them to the valley to a little town called Merced Falls that sat next to the Merced River. Nielson's flour and woolen mill were located here. The road made a sharp right turn and followed the north side of the river for seven more miles.

There was continuous green, open range as they traveled on Merced Falls Road. Finally, the family arrived at their awaited destination, the small town of Snelling!

3

Settling in Snelling

THE LAST SEVEN MILES of open range along the rushing Merced River were exciting as the whole family looked for possible sites to purchase land and build their farmhouse and barn. David and Naomi would holler and point out, "Look Mama and Papa, how 'bout over there?!" or, "Oooh, wow, what about this place?!"

But they finally arrived at a site at the corner of La Grange Road and Merced Falls Road. This was a beautiful area with a creek one mile north of the intersection. Mature oak trees dipped their roots into the little stream. The land was flat for miles and had a few rolling hills, and was only a half mile outside of Snelling. The Sawyer family set up camp and soon inquired on the property as their new homestead.

The first thing they did was to erect the two wall tents with wood-burning stoves inside for the cool autumn evenings. The animals were kept tied to nearby trees until a wood pen could be built. Jonathan planned to construct the farmhouse and barn next to the creek with the 500 acre wheat field surrounding it.

But first they had to build a three-room log cabin before the rains came. This will be their temporary home until the farmhouse was completed.

SNELLING IS A MINUTE, FRONTIER TOWN that comprised of the minimal amount of storefronts and merchants needed to keep it thriving. All the shops are located on Lewis Street, which ran the length of the town, for approximately four blocks. On this street is the Snelling Ranch Post Office, the two story Snelling County Courthouse, a livery stable on the southern end, the Snelling Meat Market on the corner of Fourth Street, Snelling's Hotel and Saloon on Third Street, and Jacobi's Store which sold provisions, groceries, wines, liquors, clothing, boots, shoes, hats, caps, crockery, glass, hardware, agricultural implements, etc. Doctor Stanley Cassidy is the only physician whose home and clinic is on Lewis Street. On the far south end of town is the Chinese Camp.

The majority of the buildings in Snelling had been remarkably reconstructed after the flood of 1862 when the Merced River overflowed its banks because of the heavy downfall of rain. The San Joaquin valley floor sustained major damage from the torrential downpour as the Sierra Mountain range contributed to the deluge of the swollen rivers. It was a miracle for the town to be back on its feet and operational within two years, but the inundation could still be seen on the exterior walls of several buildings.

AFTER A FEW DAYS OF RELAXATION at camp, Jonathan and Mary rode into town to pick up some provisions and to inquire about property. He dressed in his linen trousers with suspenders, suede vest, and slouch hat. And she put on her day dress and straw bonnet.

Their first stop was Jacobi's General Store owned by Mr. Simeon Jacobi. They tied the horse and wagon to the hitching post. Straightening her hat and dusting off her skirt, Mary checked her satchel once more for her grocery list and money. She anxiously clutched her husband's arm as he led her into the general store.

Behind the counter helping a vendor was the owner, Mr. Jacobi. The clerk, Darryl Niber was stacking jams and jellies on one of the shelves. One glance at the newcomers, Simeon excused himself to cheerfully greet his newest customers saying with a German accent, "Velcome folks! You must be new to zis area. My name is Simeon Jacobi, and za fellow over zer is Darryl. Is zere anysing we can help you wit today?"

A tall Jewish man who came from Germany, Simeon had graying blond hair which was sparse on the top of his head. He wore small round spectacles that hung on the tip of his nose as he peered down through them to read and over them to look his customers square in their eyes.

With his cheerful and friendly greeting, both Jonathan and Mary gave a sigh of relief as they glanced at each other. Jonathan extended his hand to Simeon and introduced his wife and himself.

"Yes you've guessed right, Sir. This is my wife, Mary. An' I'm Jonathan Sawyer. We arrived a few days ago by wagon train from Kentucky with our four children in hopes to settle here in Snelling. We've heard that grain farmin' is much needed in California."

Removing his glasses, cleaning it on his shirt, and placing it back on his nose, Simeon remarked and asked, "Vhy yes, more settlers are moving into zis state and food production is a necessity. Vhat types of crop are you planning on growing?"

"Wheat is what my family has farmed for several generations. I've brought seed with me, and all I need now is land, a home, an' some good farm hands."

At that moment, the lean, yet strong, middle-aged vendor of Norwegian descent, whom Simeon was attending to earlier, overheard the discussion and found himself drawn into the circle.

"Hello folks. I apologize fer listenin' to yer conversation. Allow me to introduce myself. Patrick Fay from Mount Ophir. That wagon with the oxen next to yers is mine. My line of work is farmin', and haulin' grain to Howard Nielson's flour mill in Merced Falls. There are also several China men who are acquaintances of mine that live in Snelling who are excellent farmers! Can we be of service to ya folks?" He extended a firm hand shake to Jonathan and a tilt of his worn out cowboy hat to Mary.

"Well, it appears the good Lord is guiding us into the right place and to the right people!" said Jonathan with a coy smile trying to size up Patrick Fay.

Patrick had graying black hair under his old hat. His beard was the same color and had not been trimmed for awhile.

Sweat trickled from his forehead to his brow, and he had the rugged facial features of a man who works hard. But his bright blue eyes twinkled, and he had an ear to ear grin showing his coffee stained teeth. He wore a long sleeve cotton shirt under his tattered overalls which had flour dust all over the front. Somehow Jonathan knew he would be doing business with this man.

"Yes, in fact, Patrick here was deliverin' some bags of flour from the Nielson's mill." Darryl walked over to shake their hands introducing himself. "There is plenty of land north of Snelling along the Merced River which you can purchase for 50 cents an acre. If you go to the clerk's desk at the county courthouse, she will show you a map of what is available."

"Well gentlemen. That's mighty fine news to hear. That'll be our next visit...but after my dear wife has these provisions filled." Jonathan positioned his palm on Mary's waist of her back and brought her forward.

With that, Mary handed her list to Darryl who pulled the items she needed and placed them on the counter for Simeon to tally. In the meantime, Mary found herself to be meandering towards some books on display by the store window. "Aw, *Little Folk's Delight* and also *Pictureland*! Can I start my new collection with these Jonathan?" Mary's heart flittered as she rushed to the cash register.

"Of course dear, as I promised!"

Simeon added up the provisions, "Za total comes to seven dollars and thirty cents, Mrs. Sawyer." Mary opened her satchel and counted her money and handed it to Simeon.

"Oh and by za vay...ve plan on building a school house in town. Maybe by next year dis time, dey say." Simeon made conversation.

"I do thank ya kindly for the information, Mr. Jacobi. By then, we should be settled down. For now, I am teachin' the children. What I look forward to is settlin' down and sleepin' in my own bed and cookin' food in my own kitchen!" Mary extended her hand to bid him a good day.

After Darryl and Jonathan finished loading the provisions, and Patrick unloaded the sacks of flour from his wagon, Jonathan shook their hands. Patrick scribbled on a piece of paper his address as well as the days he usually delivered.

"This is where I live, but its best ta reach me here at Mr. Jacobi's store since I'm often gone haulin' thangs throughout the area. I'll see what I can do to call on the Chinese men to work fer ya too." Patrick suggested as he handed Jonathan the sliver of paper.

"I am much obliged to ya sir!" Jonathan replied quite pleased.

Both Jonathan and Mary left Jacobi's with a sense of assurance that God wanted them to be in Snelling. Now the next step was to visit the courthouse.

MARGARET, THE COUNTY CLERK, was a pleasant and considerate older woman with faded red graying hair tied back in a bun. She wore little rectangular glasses which hugged close to her pale blue eyes. On the wall, was a map of Snelling and the Merced County line. Margaret listened to them as they inquired about the property on the corner of La Grange and Merced Falls Road where they were camped.

Jonathan removed his slouch hat as he and his wife approached Margaret's desk.

"Excuse me Ma'am. I'd like to inquire 'bout purchasing some land here in Snelling." Jonathan politely inquired.

"You're in the right place, Sir. I can help you." Margaret replied sizing up this well mannered couple with heavy Kentuckian accents.

"I am Jonathan Sawyer and this here is my wife, Mary. May I show ya on yer map where we are interested in makin' our new homestead?"

"Why certainly. That was the next thing I was going to ask you." Margaret chuckled.

So Jonathan walked over to the map on the wall and pointed to Margaret the location where they were camped. He further explained his intentions to her saying, "Our farmhouse is to be built right here and the barn over there, and this section will be 500 acres of wheat."

Margaret viewed the area and wrote down the parcel numbers and sizes until they arrived at 500 acres. With a cheerful disposition, she encouraged Jonathan and Mary. "That is a grand endeavor indeed! Yes, you may purchase those parcels at 50 cents an acre."

"Well," Jonathan replied with high hopes. "We'd like to start with 160 acres available to us through the Homestead Act. I believe there is no charge as long as I provide a note explainin' our intentions ta develop the land. Is this correct Ma'am?"

"Yes it is. You've been doin' your homework I see." Scribbling on her writing pad, Margaret chuckled.

"We will pay fer the remaining 340 acres. That should be a total of 500 acres." Jonathan did the math in his head.

"Well, let's start by having you folks take a seat, and I'll get the paperwork started and notarized."

And so Jonathan and Mary spent the remainder of the afternoon filling out forms.

"Now Mr. and Mrs. Sawyer, all you have to do is sign this deed and make your payment of $170 dollars, and the property is yours!" Margaret handed them the final documents.

With excitement, Jonathan pulled out his pocket book and paid the clerk cash, part of the proceeds from the sale of his father's farm in Perryville, Kentucky.

"Congratulations to you both! Let me shake the hands our newest citizens of Snelling!" Margaret extended them a gentle handshake and the deed.

They returned to the camp to share the good news with the children. Mary made a wonderful beef pot roast for the family to celebrate.

Sitting around the campfire, they held hands while Jonathan prayed, "Dear heavenly Father, you are the Almighty God, and we are so grateful fer yer' love and yer travelin' mercies, and getting us to our promised land, Snelling. We thank ya fer protectin' and guidin' us ev'ry step of the way, and fer yer provision in findin' this property as our new homestead. Lord we ask fer yer blessing upon this food. In Jesus' name, we pray. Amen."

And everyone shouted in unison, "Amen!"

IT TOOK A COUPLE OF DAYS of family deliberations and planning to decide the layout of the grounds. Already late September, they had to erect the three-room cabin, wood post fence, sheds for the animals and clear the land for planting before the rains came at the end of November. The barn and the farmhouse are to be built the following year.

Jonathan had brought along many of his tools from Kentucky but still needed to obtain additional lumber from the mill in Merced Falls, and order four plows and other miscellaneous items from Jacobi's store. He hired Patrick Fay to do the hauling.

Jonathan was able to hire the Chinese migrant workers whom Patrick recommended. One man named Yung was Patrick's friend, and he spoke good English, so Jonathan appointed him as the farm spokesman and interpreter. They were to help clear the trees for lumber, assist with the building projects, and plant the wheat come springtime. With their assistance, they were able to complete the cabin, wood post fencing for the corral, and the sheds for the animals by mid December…just in time for their first humble Christmas in California, the Sawyer's new homestead.

AS A HOUSEWARMING PRESENT, Patrick chopped down a little pine tree from Mariposa Grove on his way back from hauling wood for families who lived up in the foothills.

Jonathan set it in front of the window as Mary and the

children decorated sugar and gingerbread cookies for ornaments and strung popcorn and cranberries as garland. He fashioned a star from a flattened tin can with punctured nail holes that formed a star burst pattern in the center for candlelight to shine through, and welded it to another tin can with its opening facing downwards. The opened end was to be secured to the highest point of the tree. If they were extra careful, a tea candle could be placed on top of the closed end of the can behind the star and glisten through the star burst patterned holes.

The star brightly glowed, and the Christmas tree appeared absolutely delicious, beckoning the family to eat from its tasty delights.

On Christmas morning, the children awoke to find Christmas presents, which Jonathan and Mary with clever planning, found time to do as the kids were outside playing or doing their chores.

Mary had been busy making her daughters new day dresses and bonnets, and Jonathan purchased his sons some boots and a pair of Levi Strauss jeans, worn by most of the working men of California.

Jonathan graced Mary with a Victorian wide brimmed touring hat decorated with plum colored satin and plumage, black netting and lace, and a single pale pink rose. Also, included was a well tailored plum patterned day dress, trimmed with black cording, and white faux sleeves to wear under the bell shaped sleeves of her bodice.

Mary bought Jonathan a gentleman's charcoal colored Callahan frock coat, with a gray pattern double breasted Baker City vest, and a dark gray herringbone Wickham trouser.

A new home, fabulous clothes, and a renewed life! The family felt blessed by God. Before they sat down for the Christmas turkey dinner, they huddled by the wood-burning stove and Jonathan read the nativity story out loud from Luke chapter two, verse 1 through 20 in the Bible.

"In the same region there were some shepherds staying out in the fields and keeping watch over their flock by night. And an angel of the Lord suddenly stood before them, and the glory of the Lord shone around them; and they were terribly frightened. But the angel said to them, "Do not be afraid; for behold, I bring you good news of great joy which will be for all the people; for today in the city of David there has been born for you a Savior, who is Christ the Lord." This will be a sign for you: you will find a baby wrapped in cloths and lying in a manger..."

They joined hands as Jonathan said grace and gave God thanks for His blessings upon their lives that Christmas. They ate their Christmas turkey dinner and some pumpkin pie. Afterwards, they brought out their musical instruments and played Christmas carols all night long before bedtime.

4

The First Harvest

I T IS NOW FEBRUARY 1865, and most of the rainy season had passed. Jonathan, Samuel, Patrick, and the Chinese farmhands took advantage of the damp soil to begin plowing up the first 250 acres of field, and trenching the irrigation ditches which tapped into the creek. Mary, Sarah, Naomi, and David came behind them and broadcast the wheat seed. The family has to finish plowing and planting by May with the aim of harvesting the initial crop in July and complete by late August.

As he plowed, Jonathan became aware of what seemed to be either cow or buffalo chips. This had concerned Jonathan even though the excrement is good for fertilization. At this time, most of the San Joaquin Valley was public domain and the cattle were allowed to freely graze without restrictions. Jonathan's concern is whether or not the cattlemen knew he had purchased this land.

By late April, the first 250 acres of wheat had grown at

least six inches tall. When Jonathan and Samuel headed early in the morning towards the corral to prepare the horses for plowing, Jonathan heard the unusual sound of cattle lowing in the distance. Jonathan glanced up and scanned the crops and to his dismay over a dozen cows stood grazing on the wheat along the northern wayside.

"Oh no, no, no!" Jonathan said out loud. "Sam, get our guns. Cattle are in the field. I'll fetch Fire and Jake."

So Samuel ran into the cabin, grabbed their gun belts and met Jonathan outside to saddle their horses. They rode with haste over to the field's edge and did their best to scare them off by shooting into the air. By the time they had scared them away, much of the sprouts had been trodden upon and eaten.

Jonathan dismounted his horse to survey the damage done. He crouched down to examine the trampled seedling and the stubble that remained.

"Dang them cattle!" Jonathan cursed under his breath as he plucked his damaged produce from the ground. After examining it, he threw it down with disgust. "What a darn shame. This is gonna cost us."

This infuriated Jonathan, so he went to the courthouse on the 15th of April to file a complaint with the Justice of Peace, Marshall Robert Warner who is a stocky man. His dark shoulder length hair rested on the collar of his charcoal grey frock coat. His black slouch hat hung on the wall behind his desk, and his ebony spurred boots could be heard jangling whenever he walked about.

Upon Jonathan's arrival, excitement and chatter electrified the room with the news regarding President Lincoln's assassination. The telegraph came in by Morse code. The eastern and western halves of the United States had been brought closer together through this little device made available to California in 1861.

Margaret, the county clerk, read the message coming from the San Francisco County office, "President Abraham Lincoln Shot in head. Stop. April 14th. Stop. Died this morning. Stop. Assassin at large. Stop."

Pandemonium filled the courtroom after hearing this report. They gathered around Margaret trying to take it from her hand to read for themselves. Because he could not calm anyone down, Marshall Warner grabbed his Colt revolver, packed it with powder, and shot towards the ceiling. The gun made a loud blast which rang in the ears of the people that quieted them down immediately.

"Listen folks!" The Marshall bellowed. "Settle down. Once we receive more news, I will have Margaret post it on the front door. In the meantime, inform your family and friends of this tragic incident and keep the President, his wife, and our country in your prayers! Please get business done here and go home, and do not involve yourself in any rioting or unlawful conduct because of this situation. Thank you folks!"

Jonathan did his best to discuss his grievance, despite the inattentive response he received.

"Marshall Warner," Jonathan began as the Marshall returned to his desk. "I'd like to file a complaint against whoever owned the livestock grazing on my property. Do you know who these cattle belong to?" Jonathan huffed pointing towards his farm.

Leaning back on his chair, the Marshall's facial countenance expressed his thoughts to be, "Are you kidding me?" He replied sarcastically, "Well, they are owned by Jackson Montana one of the wealthiest cattlemen in California. He is also one of the superintendants of Merced County."

Because of the politics involved and the timing of the President's assassination, Jonathan perceived that his complaint fell short on the priority list.

"Excuse me Sir. Much time and money has been lost on damaged crop. I don't care if he is the President of the United States. Damage is damage, and there must be a law which protects property owners caused by someone else's neglect!" Jonathan exclaimed.

Aggravated, Marshall Warner threw his hands upward. "Alright! Alright! You've got every right to complain," he agreed with the purpose of getting Jonathan out of his way, so he could move on with other business.

"Here ya go. Fill out this complaint form and return it to Margaret and she'll notify Jackson Montana," replying with slack intentions.

Jonathan filed the grievance to no avail because of the politics involved and the timing of the bad news about President Lincoln taking precedence. In addition, California did not have enough law officials, resulting in the wealthy cattle owners having the advantage at this time. Much of justice had to be dealt with through the integrity of the individuals. In other words, each individual had to take the law into his or her own hands.

WELL, THIS SITUATION PUT A DELAY in the planting process. The farmhands spent the next few weeks building a fence around the 500 acres to keep livestock from grazing in the field. But before this could be completed the cattle kept returning.

One morning while trying to chase them away, Samuel found himself to be challenged by a bull. It clawed at the dirt and began to charge at Samuel and his horse, Fire. With immediate accuracy, Jonathan shot the bull which tumbled to the ground destroying more crops because of its weight and inertia moving forward before it died.

Patrick Fay, who himself owned a small stock of cattle, rode over to the carcass to check its branding. Examining it, he recognized the brand marks as belonging to Jackson Montana, confirming Marshall Warner's suspicion.

"Well, boss, there's nothin' much ya could do." Patrick reassured Jonathan and further justified his deed saying, "It's either the bull or yer son."

"This ought ta get the cattleman's attention," Jonathan said with reluctance. "In the meantime, let's butcher it an' we can share it amongst ourselves."

So the men secured a lasso around its neck and tied the rope to the horn of their saddles and dragged it near the corral where they butchered.

Later on in the day, the Vaqueros, Jackson Montana's cattlemen, rustled about town looking for their bull. News regarding the Sawyer's trouble with the cattle grazing in the fields had spread amongst the towns people.

Riding along La Grange Road, the Vaqueros headed for the Sawyers farm and became aware for the first time that much of the land had been cleared and had heads of wheat growing in neatly planted rows, bordered by a wood post fence which had not been completed. They also observed that some of the crops had been disturbed and found the pool of blood where the bull had been shot.

"Aye, yi, yi…dis is not good, Juan," said Miguel as he peered down at the evidence on the ground..

"Si…we better go talk to the owner," exclaimed Juan nervously.

So they both rode over to the cabin with caution, sensing trouble for the damage caused by the cattle. They did not know what to expect from these new residence, especially since they shot the bull. The Vaqueros tucked their colt revolvers under their ponchos, straightened their sombreros, and they knocked on the door as the Sawyer family sat down for their evening meal.

A sinking feeling knotted up in Jonathan, Mary, and Samuel's stomachs. A rush of adrenaline filled Jonathan's veins knowing trouble was brewing. So both he and Samuel grabbed their gun belts and put them on in case they needed them. Mary, Sarah, Naomi, and David rushed into the bedroom to listen with patience and wait for the outcome of this strange and uninvited knock.

Opening the door slowly, Jonathan found two hefty Vaqueros standing on the front porch intensely staring him in the eye. "How can I help ya fellers?" said Jonathan with disdain.

"Excuse us Senior, but we are Senior Montana's Vaqueros. We are missing one of our bulls, and someone in town told us that you might know where it is," explained Miguel.

"Well, it so happens we had some unwelcomed visits from several of yer cattle the last few weeks. We found them to be trampling all over a big portion of our wheat an' destroyed much of the crop. We did our best to scare them away from our land; however, they kept returning one day after another. Just today your bull came charging at my son, so I had no option but to shoot him down." Jonathan explained with anger in his voice.

"Please inform Senior Montana I am taking his bull an' any of his cattle, which graze on my land, as payment fer the damage of crops. Should he have difficulty with this proposal, he may come an' see me an' we'll settle this in another fashion. If I were ya fellers, I would do all you can to make sure the cattle do not trespass on this property." Jonathan asserted.

"Gracias, Senior Sawyer. We will inform him of what happened here," replied Miguel.

The two Vaqueros mounted their steeds and with swiftness rode back to where they had the cattle grazing. Juan would ride out to Jackson Montana's ranch in Bear Creek informing him of the situation the next morning.

THE NEWS DID NOT SETTLE WELL with Jackson Montana. At age 51, he became the richest cattleman in the San Joaquin Valley with over 10,000 heads of cattle. Being an old Kentuckian himself, people understood him to be fair, honest and kind. He owned 640 acres of land mostly near his ranch, and also purchased 40 acre parcels around most of the watering holes in the region of Merced.

More of his cattlemen came to him with this type of news as

grain farmers bought the best grazing land in central California. He was beginning to lose head of cattle to the agriculturalist.

"I am not certain that I agree with Mr. Sawyer's proposal. Ya boys make sure the cattle do not trespass on his land. If anymore head are missing, tell me immediately. Comprende?" commanded Jackson Montana as he pushed away from his office desk and crossed over to the parlor window to admire his livestock. He lit a cigar, took a long, slow drag, and exhaled.

"Should this happen again I might be forced to take some kind of action," he exclaimed as he thought of how he could settle this matter in case another incident occur.

"Si, Senor Montana. We will do our best to keep the cattle away from the Sawyer Ranchero. Adios, Senor," replied Miguel as he nervously turned on the heel of his boot and headed outside of the Montana ranch house and rode back to Snelling.

FOR THE REMAINING PLANTING SEASON, no more incidents occurred as the Vaqueros pushed the cattle east of Snelling to graze. Building the wood post fence added delay to the schedule, but they were able to finish about a week behind.

New problems would trouble Jonathan. His observation of the crop planted inland on very rocky ground grew fast. When the sun really started heating up, sometimes to 105 degrees in June, the crops withered and died.

The next problem he encountered is the stalks planted nearest the river where much of the wild pine, oak trees, and raspberries grew. The roots of those plants had not been properly extracted and they started growing back, resulting in the wheat being crowded out.

Jonathan became discouraged and resorted to patiently waiting for the results of the damages. Perhaps, he thought to himself, he had been over ambitious in trying to plant the entire 500 acres on land which has never been farmed before.

With shoulders down, Jonathan entered the cabin and sat down at the kitchen table and placed his cowboy hat on the chair next to him. He leaned back and stared at Mary who was stirring the stew on the wood-burning stove. She watched Jonathan enter the room and had discerned that he was not his normal jovial self.

"What's wrong, honey?" Mary asked knowing her husband appeared troubled.

"I am not sure, Mary. I don't think this first harvest is gonna do well fer us this year. Not only is there damage from the cattle, but part of the crop withered an' died, an' another section is overwhelmed by weeds. All our hard work an' I think we're gonna barely break even," Jonathan said downcast.

"Now don't ya worry John. We both believed that God wanted us to move out here. We need to trust Him for His provision. Maybe this ain't the best year, but this is only yer first. Don't give up already. There's much to be thankful fer, thanks to the good Lord!" Mary encouraged Jonathan.

"The children and I love bein' here. We've met some fine people, and it's all been a blessin' so far. God never promised an easy path. You need to be patient and wait on the Lord," Mary exclaimed.

"Yep yer right Mary. You knew exactly what I needed to

hear. Maybe I'm just tired from pushin' myself too hard and workin' non-stop since we arrived here. I haven't had much time to sit down an' pray and thank God, and ask Him fer His help or His strength. This is what's missin' in my life. I've gotten so busy I've forgotten who is in control. Yer correct as always, Mary. I need to trust God more," Jonathan agreed and felt resolve to his recent worries.

JUNE WAS A SLOW MONTH, so the men worked on building the barn while Jonathan found a moment to relax, peruse the Bible, and spend time with the Lord in prayer.

He read about Job and how God allowed Satan to test his faith and love for Him. The enemy took everything from Job; his home, his family and even his health. Job continued to acknowledge and trust God's judgment and goodness despite his misfortune. In the end, God restored all that Job had because of his faithfulness.

Jonathan thought to himself, "Perhaps God is testing my faith in Him." He knew that he had to remain faithful even if the first crop did not do as well as he had hoped. Jonathan was not aware this was one test amongst many of his faith in God.

JULY AND AUGUST would be the months to reap the wheat. With the help of Patrick and the Chinese migrant workers, Jonathan and Samuel finished building the barn in June.

The harvest turned out to be a disappointment for Jonathan as twenty-five percent of the crops damaged by the cattle never recovered. In addition to this, ten percent of the crop along the stony ground grew rapidly into maturity, but died in the hot sun for lack of good soil and not developing deep roots. Yet another ten percent did not grow well next to the river because weeds overwhelmed the wheat.

The remaining fifty-five percent was harvested and bundled, thrown in wagons, and hauled over several trips to Nielsen's Flour Mill in Merced Falls.

The milling factory stood close to the Merced River using the natural forces of the rushing water to provide energy to move the heavy grinding wheel. Next to the mill are two grain silos with a long ladder used for baling and separating the chaff, and the three-story warehouse and office facility stood next to it.

Harold Nielson, the owner, sat behind his oak desk with Jonathan sitting across him waiting for the final measurement of the wheat. The foreman walked into the office and handed him a piece of paper showing the weight of the grain. So he calculated the purchase price from the Sawyer's Farm.

"You have 330 tons of wheat, Mr. Sawyer. Minus one third returned to you is 220 tons, which I will buy from you. My going rate is thirty dollars a ton. So that'll come to $6,600." The owner calculated from behind his desk.

"Thank ya, Mr. Nielson. Next year I plan on doubling this amount and doin' better. This is our first harvest of wheat on virgin land, and we ran into some problems," Jonathan explained.

"Well I'll be ready for you," Mr. Nielson replied as he handed Jonathan a note for $6,600 and shook hands. "Thank you for your business."

The mill threshed the wheat and one third of the seed had been returned to Jonathan for planting the following year. The remaining was heaved into a long elevator where the chaff is to be baled and be ground into flour, bagged then delivered to the general stores or bakeries. Jonathan made some profit from his first crop, but not nearly what he had hoped for. He still praised God and thanked Him for His goodness and His provision for his family.

5

The Camp Meeting

FTER THE DISCOURAGING HARVEST in late August, Pastor Daniel McSwan and his wife, Ruth, made a timely visit to the Sawyer Farm. The farmhands finished their work for the day and returned to their homes.

Pastor McSwan and Ruth rode up to the farm in their horse and buggy as Jonathan and Samuel led the horses into the barn. After they had parked by the cabin, he jumped out as Ruth stayed seated, holding the reins.

He straightened his cravat and adjusted his grey colored vest and linen frock coat, dusted off his dark trousers, and put on his black planter flat crown hat over his silvery blond, short cropped hair.

He walked over to the open barn doors and cleared his throat. "Hello! Is anyone home?"

"Hey Pa, are you expectin' someone?" Samuel whispered to his father while he closed the horse's stall gate.

"Nope. Not that I know of." Jonathan quietly replied looking at the shadowed figure standing in the opening of the barn door with the sun setting low behind him.

"Who's inquiring?" Jonathan called out as he put the harnesses away.

"Good day to you Sir! My name is Pastor Daniel McSwan. I've come to introduce myself to you and invite you to a camp meeting!" He threw his voice into the dimly lit barn.

Realizing this is a friendly visitation both Jonathan and Samuel proceeded towards the sunlit door and extended a hand shake to Pastor McSwan.

"How do ya do, Pastor? I am Jonathan Sawyer, an' this is my first born son, Samuel. Welcome to our farm!"

"I'm doing well, thank you. I finally made a point to ride out here with my wife, Ruth, to meet you folks. I'll be preaching the entire weekend starting on Friday, September 8th through Sunday, September 10th at Branche's Ferry, on the Tuolumne, a short distance below La Grange. I realize it's about ten miles from your farm, but I figure since the harvest is almost over, a relaxing retreat might be enjoyable for you all," persuaded Pastor McSwan.

Mary, Sarah, Naomi, and David came scurrying out of the cabin towards the barn. "Speaking of family…Pastor an' Mrs. McSwan, please meet my wife Mary, daughters, Sarah who is fourteen, Naomi who is ten, an' our youngest son David who is nine years old." A flurry of hand shakes and warm welcomes were exchanged.

"Pastor and his lovely wife are inviting us to a camp meetin' in a couple of weekends from today in La Grange. Now that the harvest is over, suppose we get away an' go have some fun before school starts!"

"Oh Papa, can we please?!" The children cheered and jumped for joy.

The Sawyer family recalled the camp meetings, also known as brush arbor meetings, they attended back in Kentucky. Between late Spring and early Fall, traveling ministers or evangelists would locate an open field outside of town to preach. Makeshift arbors had been erected to provide shade for the people coming to listen. Tall and thin trees are cut down and the top or brushy parts removed so the trunk could be used as poles. Four poles are set in the ground to make a square and cross poles are attached to the top. The brush that had been removed is placed on top of the cross poles creating a shady area for the campers.

Benches are made by attaching planks of wood atop two or three wooden vegetable crates. The children disliked those benches because parents behind them noticed any mischief and whispered in their ears to be still or gave them a pinch to pay attention. The benches are hard, uncomfortable and difficult to sit in too long. The little ones would get fidgety looking at people's backs in front of them, especially if a lady wore a big hat and blocked their view of the Pastor. The sermons were always lengthy and loud and the children quickly became frustrated and bored.

The camp meetings became an annual social event for relatives and friends from all over the county to visit one another. The environment was safe and family friendly, so the children were allowed to roam free to play while the parents socialized. This was also an opportunity for singles to find their significant other. On the last evening, the families brought baskets of food to share and place on blankets on the ground.

Music and laughter filtered through the air and added to the camp meeting fun.

"Well, Pastor, I believe you can be expectin' our family to be present as we have not found a church to attend yet in these parts," Jonathan replied. "And to tell ya the truth, I've been feelin' quite thirsty and faint of late, if ya know what I mean. It's been too long since we've been ta church and have sensed the touch of God in our lives."

"Praise be to God!" The Pastor was elated. "I also preach every Sunday at nine o'clock in the morning, during the late fall and winter months at the county courthouse in Snelling. You folks are welcomed to join us. But in the spring and summer I conduct the camp meetings in several foothill counties. I enjoy bringing the Gospel of good news to people living in remote areas."

"Lord willing, we will be able to attend those meetings too." Mary looked over to the Pastor nodding her head. "By the way, we are about to sit down to have supper. We would love to have you to stay awhile!"

"Oh my! How thoughtful of you, Mrs. Sawyer. Normally we'd take up your offer, but it is getting late and we have one more visit to make before dark. Thank you though. Perhaps we might arrange another day to have dinner together." Ruth respectfully dismissed herself.

Ruth was a graceful, medium framed lady, slightly older than Mary. She had silky strawberry blond hair fashioned in fine ringlets under her wide brimmed straw touring hat trimmed with white satin ribbon, netting, and wild flowers. She wore a beautiful gold printed day dress with a hoop skirt which spread out over the seat of the buggy.

"Well, I will leave you with this parchment with the details of the camp meeting. We look forward to seeing you folks and spending some time with you!" Pastor McSwan handed the sheet of paper to Jonathan, shook his hand, and hopped back into the buggy. Naomi and David chased them to the end of the drive as they waved them good-bye.

THE TWO WEEKS since the McSwan's visit went by too slow as the Sawyer family anxiously waited for the event. The wagon was packed and ready to go on Thursday, September 7th. The four days included the travel day going to La Grange and coming home on Sunday, since Naomi and David had to start school in Snelling the following Monday, September 11th. It actually started on September 4th, the previous Monday. But because of the camp, Mary decided to enroll the children after their return.

They arrived at Branche's Ferry in the late afternoon, in time to set up and prepare supper. Pastor McSwan and his family greeted them and directed them to their camp site. Two large circles of wagons formed one inside the other around the wood platform stage in the center. Inside the circle were several brush arbors.

"I'm so glad to have you here, folks! You all remember my wife, Ruth."

Pastor McSwan turned to his wife, who reached over to Mary and gave her a big hug. "Now you can meet our children.

This is Joshua who is fifteen and Rebecca who is eight years old."

Joshua is a well mannered young man, timid, but not shy. The ends of his neatly cut brownish blond hair shown under his dark cap. He wore a yellow and russet cotton plaid shirt, brown linen trousers, and suspender.

"Hello, welcome to camp!" Greeting the family first, as his eyes met with Sarah's, who then began to blush.

Rebecca is a sweet, but spunky gal with gold ringlets tied into a ponytail. She had on a cotton printed day dress which came above her shins. The lace of her pant drawer was visible as it covered her ankles in her muddy black boots. Out of breath from running around the camp with other children her age, she impatiently greeted, "Hi there!" and turned to her father, "Can I go play now, Father?"

"Well, wait a minute young lady. Why don't you take Naomi and David with you…that is if it's all right with their Mama and Papa." Pastor McSwan clutched his daughter's hand and looked toward Jonathan and Mary.

"I don't have any objections," Mary exclaimed. "They'll be in the way while we are pitchin' camp anyways."

Mary then turned to her two youngest with a stern warning. "Children…be in yer best behavior. Try not to get yer clothes too dirty. We'll be eatin' supper in about an hour. So be back in time to wash up, ya hear!"

Rebecca smiled and grabbed their hands, "Come on. We're making a may pole down by the river." The children then scurried away giggling.

Pastor McSwan turned to his son to volunteer him. "Joshua, why don't you help these good folks set up camp while your mother and I continue to direct the other people arriving?"

"Sure Father."

Joshua turned to Jonathan. "Just show me what I need to do Mr. Sawyer."

He brushed by Sarah whom he sensed had her eyes fixed on him. The Sawyer's went to work directing the three youth. Sarah and Joshua kept glancing at each other every moment they could find while they worked.

"Samuel. Why don't ya set up the stove and gather some wood to start a fire." Jonathan instructed. "Joshua, would you mind helpin' me to put up this canopy by the side of the wagon fer shade?"

"I wouldn't mind at all, Sir." Joshua said politely.

"Sarah, you can help me by huskin' the corn and puttin out plates, while I start makin' the fried chicken an' biscuits." Mary handed Sarah a basket of corn.

"Okay, Ma!" Sarah grabbed the basket and looked over to Joshua who was separating wood poles, ropes, and stakes for the canopy.

Sarah's soft brown hair is parted down the middle, braided on each side and pulled back in a bun. She wore a straw hat which had a matching bow as the material of her day dress.

This is the first time she had met anybody or noticed any boy her age since they left Kentucky. She had never experienced this warm sensation before as her heart began beating fast in her chest.

With their chores finished, Joshua bid goodnight to the family and met eyes once again with Sarah. "I'll see everyone tomorrow!"

AT NINE O'CLOCK IN THE MORNING, the people brought their blankets to the center lawn area around the stage to sit and sing worship songs and listen to the sermon under the brush arbor. A two-hour break for lunch and dinner provided enough social time in between sermons. The evenings were open to those who desired to pray and worship all night, or as long as they wanted. The real pious of the faith worshipped till the sun came up, and break for breakfast and get a quick "shut eye", and start again at nine the next morning.

The next two days became a milestone for the Sawyer family as they experienced a spiritual awakening in their lives. They worshipped God and sang hymns from the Camp Meeting Chorister hymnal. *"Come all ye weary travelers. Great God, where'er we pitch our tent. How pleasant are these tents oh Lord"*…etc.

They enjoyed every Spirit inspired word Pastor McSwan spoke. Even Naomi and David understood what salvation through Jesus Christ meant.

"If you have not received Jesus Christ as your Lord and Savior, then I want you to come to the altar and I will pray with you." Pastor McSwan encouraged those who heard the Gospel message for the first time.

"The Lord is tugging at your heart telling you He loves you. Confess to Him and He will forgive you of your sins and grant you everlasting life." Pastor McSwan continued to preach, and many people came to the wooden stage platform.

He opened the hymnal book and sang. *"Come all ye weary*

travelers..." as more congregated in front.

Suddenly, the four children went forward. The children's salvation meant the world to Jonathan and Mary, and tears of joy swelled up in their eyes as the pastor prayed for them and welcomed them into God's family.

Pastor McSwan addressed the new Believers, "Now, all you have to do is recite after me this simple prayer of faith... Heavenly Father..."

The people repeated after him, "Heavenly Father."

"I come to you asking for the forgiveness of my sins. I confess with my mouth and believe with my heart that Jesus is your Son and that he died on the cross at Calvary that I might be forgiven and have eternal life in the Kingdom of Heaven. Father, I believe that Jesus rose from the dead and I ask you to come into my life and be my personal Lord and Savior. I repent of my sins and will worship you all the days of my life! Because your word is truth, I confess with my mouth that I am born again, and cleansed by the blood of Jesus! In Jesus name, Amen..." Pastor prayed, and the new Believers repeated the prayer quietly to themselves.

This happened while Sarah kept looking out for Joshua who had been busy working at the camp meeting.

SUNDAY MORNING ARRIVED sooner than they had hoped. The event continued one more day, but the Sawyer family had to return home since school was about to start.

Leaving became difficult knowing the Holy Spirit was working divinely in the lives of their children and in the other Believers around them.

They said their final farewells to Pastor McSwan and his family, and Sarah tried her best to bury her feelings should she never see Joshua again as they met eyes for the last time. She simply smiled and climbed into the wagon. Their ride back home passed quickly because they chattered on about the weekend and sang their favorite hymns along the way.

6

School for Naomi and David

MARY AND JONATHAN AGREED that Naomi who is ten, and David nine, should attend Snelling School. Sarah who is now fourteen and Samuel, who is sixteen, were needed around the farm since much of their education had already been completed through Mary.

Mary, Naomi, and David woke early Monday morning to prepare for the first day of school. Desiring to meet the new teacher, Mary donned on her day dress and straw hat. She would walk with Naomi, who wore an ordinary olive green printed day dress and bonnet, and David, wearing his linen gray trousers with suspenders over a pale blue plaid shirt and cap. She filled two small baskets with a chicken salad sandwich, an apple, and a cookie for their lunches and covered it with a cloth napkin.

The school is located at the edge of town closest to the farm and is an easy half mile walk from the cabin by walking along the wayside path of the wheat field.

"Come on David! Don't dawdle!" Mary tried hurrying him as he was reluctant to attend school. "Tie yer boot laces the both of ya! We have to leave now before we're late."

Class started at 8:30 in the morning but Mary, Naomi and David arrived at 8:15, enough time to meet Mr. Cavern, Snelling's first instructor.

The brand new schoolhouse is painted an eggshell white with brick-red trim on the shutters and door. David swung the door open for Mary and Naomi, who delighted in the cheerful, well lit one-room class.

It had two large windows on the left and right side of the classroom, allowing sunlight to filter in. Under the windows are low-book shelves. Between the two windows on the left side is a large color painting of George Washington in a dark brown wood frame on the wall. Between the two windows on the right is a hanging map of the world, also in the same colored frame.

There are two rows of five, two-person wood and metal student desks, efficiently arranged which filled the room. The classroom smelled of fresh paint, and the desks and chairs had a warm honey glow.

Mr. Cavern's molasses brown, chestnut desk is positioned in the front to the left. Stacked in three piles is about two dozen books called *The New England Primer* which would be given to each student as their text book. There is also a Bible, an ink well and pen, and a box of pencils. At the left corner, behind him are the United States flag and staff.

To the front right corner is a stool with a dunce hat for the student who needed some disciplining. Slightly to the front of that is a black iron wood-burning stove to keep the room warm in the winter.

Behind the teachers desk is a large blackboard centered on the wall with his name written in chalk and the message, "Welcome to Snelling Grade School!"

Mr. Cavern is about in his forties and is a discreet and unobtrusive gentleman. He wore a white linen shirt, a gray-blue Crocker vest, and jacket with matching trousers, and a western bow tie. His dark hair is cut short, parted to the left side, and curled at the ends.

Mary and the children walked into the classroom. Seated at his desk writing, he looked up and peered at them over his reading spectacles.

"Hello Madam, students," he greeted as he rose from his chair, bowed and extended his hand to shake Mary's. He had proper mannerisms and articulate speech. "My name is Mr. Cavern. Welcome to Snelling School."

"Good morning to ya, Mr. Cavern. I am Mrs. Sawyer of Sawyer Farm. We live around the corner, on La Grange Road. These are two of my four children, Naomi an' David, come to join Snelling School! The two eldest, Samuel an' Sarah, have completed their education an' are a big help at home."

"Ah yes. I am familiar with your farm and family, from a distance that is. From my classroom window, I can get a glimpse of you working diligently on the field. I had been wondering when you would be attending school, children. Well, I am most certainly glad to have you as my pupils this first year, Naomi and David! Please find a seat in the classroom and we will begin class in a few minutes."

Suddenly the school house door opened and about a dozen students rushed in noisily, chattering and greeting Mr. Cavern, placing an apple or fruit on his desk, and scurrying to their seats.

Mary crouched to give her children a hug. "Well my dear ones, I will see you at the farm when school is over."

She stood saying, "Thank ya an' good day, Mr. Cavern. It is splendid to meet ya." She exited the classroom, closing the door behind her.

Meanwhile, Sarah had finished milking the cow and began feeding the chickens and gathering eggs; as Samuel, Boomer, and Ann rustled the horses and oxen to the fields to graze on the remaining wheat stubble.

Jonathan was in the cabin working on the plans for the farmhouse when Mary came home.

"How'd the children do with their new teacher?" Jonathan asked Mary.

"Oh they did just fine. Mr. Cavern seems to be a gentle and self-controlled soul. I think they will enjoy his teachin'."

She wrapped her apron around her waist to begin the process of making bread. She pulled the jar of flour from the top shelf of the wood framed pantry which Jonathan had built for the dry goods. She also grabbed yeast, salt, oil and sugar and mixed all the ingredients in a bowl and started kneading it into dough. Afterwards, she placed it in a greased bowl, and covered with a damp towel and allowed it to rise to double its size.

While Mary was preparing the meals for the day, Patrick pulled up to the barn in his wagon, jumped out and went looking for Samuel.

"Hey Sam...how'd you like to help me deliver some sacks of flour and barley the next few days to the general stores in Coulterville, Chinese Camp, and Jamestown?" Patrick's gruff sounding voice bellowed.

Samuel was elated with the opportunity, especially upon

hearing about going to Jamestown.

"You bet I'd like to go!" Samuel replied with a big grin.

"Well, let's ask yer Pa, and Ma. We'll probably be gone a li'l more than a week, so you'll have to pack a few thangs like a blanket, a mattress, an' a warm coat. We'll be camping along the way, so bring yer shot gun so we can do some huntin'!" Patrick exclaimed wide eyed, slapping his knee with his right hand.

Patrick and his wife had one son, but he died of cholera on September 24, 1859. That was a difficult time for both he and Ingrid, and continues to be. They have found solace in God and the promise of one day seeing their son again in heaven. Hauling and delivering product from one town to another helped him to keep from thinking about the death of his son. It was healing for him to have Samuel around, and he grew extremely fond of him as if he were his own child.

So they both walked over to the cabin, to talk to Jonathan and Mary.

"Good day to ya folks!" Patrick greeted as he sat himself down at the table where Jonathan was working.

"Well howdy, Pat! Nice of ya to drop by. How's thangs goin' for ya?" Jonathan continued working on the farmhouse drawings.

"John, ya know this is a busy time of the year fer me deliverin' grain to the general stores in our county. Sure could use some assistance, and I'm hopin' you would allow me to borrow Sam to help fer 'bout nine days to deliver in the foothill towns of Coulterville, Chinese Camp, an' Jamestown. I'll give him a handsome wage if he'll lend me a hand!" Patrick laid his straw hat on the kitchen table and wiped the sweat from his brow.

Jonathan paused for a moment, looked over to Mary who

stopped kneading the dough and locked her eyes with his, searching for an answer.

"Don't look at me John. You'll have to make that decision. This would be a good time fer Sam to go since the harvest is over. I suppose, between you, Sarah, an' I, we can manage his chores for a week," Mary suggested but left the decision up to Jonathan.

Jonathan realized that Sam is a hard worker and is always at his beckoning call. Sam had an opportunity to be responsible for making his own decisions without their aid. This moment may be advantageous for him since he is soon to be an adult.

"Hum." Jonathan placed his elbows on the kitchen table, folded his hands and brought it under his chin. "Do ya think ya can handle it on yer own, son, an' take instruction from Pat as yer employer?"

"Yes Sir Pa! I'll do anything he tells me to do!" Samuel replied with enthusiasm.

"Well Pat…he is all yers…for nine days that is. You'll probably be camping, so how would you like to bring Boomer along with ya boys?" Jonathan was thinking of their added protection.

"I cain't thank you enough, John! Yes, we'll take Boomer with us, and Sam's rifle in case we plan on doin' some huntin'… if that's all right with you of course?"

"Sure why not. You may need it for protection too, an' Sam knows how to handle his guns well." Jonathan beamed with pride for his son.

"Okay, I have to make a delivery to town today, then I'll come back in the mornin' to pick ya up, Sam, with yer thangs." Patrick shook Jonathan's hand and gave Samuel a pat on his shoulder.

"Thank ya too, Mary! Good day to y'all!" grinned Patrick as he exited the cabin and climbed back into his wagon and left for town.

After finishing his chores, Samuel collected the things he needed for the hauling journey. He rolled up his feather mattress, gum blanket, and Mary's old, thick quilt. Packed in a canvas sack are one linen shirt, his long underwear, and a heavy wool coat. He wore his slouch hat, a red scarf bandana around his neck, and his boots. Around his hip is the Colt revolver and gun belt, and his rifle was in its leather sleeve.

Naomi and David returned home in the late afternoon and could not stop chattering about the friends they met and the new things they learned. They felt relieved to know that Rebecca McSwan also attended.

"Okay y'all…supper is ready, so why don't ya wash up, an' we'll discuss everythang at the kitchen table!" Hollering at the children, Mary arranged the dishes on the table as Jonathan removed his work.

They sat down, and Jonathan prayed, "Dear Lord, we thank ya fer yer provisions fer our family, an' fer this delicious food prepared by the loving hands of my wife. Bless it now to nourish our bodies. Amen…Let's eat!"

As the meal was passed around the table, Samuel, Naomi, and David cheerfully shared their happy news, as Mary and Jonathan interjected comments and parental guidance.

Samuel started. "I'm gonna be gone 'bout nine days with Patrick to deliver bags of flour and barley to some general stores in the foothills. Can y'all cover me on my chores 'til I get back? If you'd do me this favor, I promise I'll do one fer you one day," Samuel petitioned his brother and sisters.

"Samuel, don't make any promises ya cain't keep," Mary advised. "We're family here, and we are ta help one another out unconditionally, as long as it is fer somethin' good, and not evil."

"Well, I would appreciate if y'all can cover me till I'm back." Samuel corrected himself.

"This'll be grand! We'll be goin' to Jamestown. Do y'all remember the gold prospectors? Maybe Patrick and I will have time to do some pannin' while we're there." Samuel said with high hopes as he picked at his dinner.

"Well, if ya strike it rich Sam, I expect ya to remember yer promise to pay us back!" Sarah chuckled.

"What 'bout you two, Naomi and David? How was yer first day of school?" Jonathan asked with immense curiosity.

"It kinda started out scary." David fidgeted and stared at his plate. "Then Rebecca saw us and sat right next ta us, and I wasn't afraid after that. I thought Mr. Cavern was gonna be mean, but he is a real swell teacher, and he's teachin' us our alphabet by memorizin' thangs from the Bible."

"Yah...like what?" Mary asked curiously. "Why don't ya recite somethin' David."

"Well," David tried to recollect. "A...In Adam's fall, we sinned all. B...Heaven to find, the Bible mind. And C... And C..."

"And C...Christ crucified, for sinners died." Naomi rudely interrupted her little brother.

"You showoff." David retorted.

"How 'bout you Naomi? What did you enjoy best today?" Jonathan asked.

"I met three new girl friends my age. Their names are Ruby, Della and Abigail. The thang I enjoyed bes' 'bout school is recess and lunch break." Naomi said with a wise cracker tone of voice as she chomped on her green beans.

"Now Naomi," Mary had to reprimand her head strong daughter. "You better had paid good attention to yer schooling, 'less ya wanna grow up ta be beggin' on the streets somewhere."

"I know ma. I know. Ya told me that a hundred times." Naomi sassed back.

"Young lady. If I hear ya talkin' to your Ma like that one more time, you'll get the rod. Ya hear me!?" Jonathan snapped, pointing his index finger at Naomi. "Now, you apologize to yer' Ma."

"Sorry, Ma, I'll pay better attention at school."

Listening to her brothers and sister, Sarah felt a little neglected as she sat quietly at the dinner table with the family.

Sensing this, Mary suggested to Sarah, "Sarah, since Naomi an' David will be in school, an' Samuel gone fer a week, why don't you an' I go into town tomorrow an' pick up some material to make ya a new dress. Pastor McSwan told me that he will be preachin' at the county courthouse two Sundays from now. I thought we all ought to go to hear him again once Sam is back."

This brought a smile to Sarah's long face. "Okay Mama. I would love that!" Sarah said as her mood changed, sat up straight, and finished her dinner. Sarah tried her best to enter into the conversation with her brothers and sisters and encourage them in their new endeavors. The thoughts of the possibility of seeing Joshua also danced in her mind.

7

Samuel Tempted by Gold

THE NEXT DAY, Tuesday morning, at eight o'clock, Patrick came by to pick up Samuel and Boomer, for the week-long hauling of flour to the general stores in the Sierra Mountain foothill mining towns.

"Mornin' folks!" Patrick said cheerfully looking forward to having Samuel come along. "Thank ya again fer allowin' Sam to help me out!"

"Ya ready ta go Sam?" Patrick looked over at Sam as he grabbed his belongings.

"Mornin' Pat! Yep I'm ready when you are!" Samuel replied.

"All right, you can throw yer thangs in the back of the wagon." Patrick instructed.

Samuel gave his family hugs and whistled for Boomer. "Come on Boomer!"

They all climbed into the wagon and slowly rode down the drive.

"Oh Lord. This is his first time away from us." Mary prayed

out loud to herself, "Father please watch after them and bring them home safely."

Jonathan stood by her waving them goodbye. "Amen. The farm is gonna seem strange without him aroun'."

"Yep, I already can sense it," A tremble could be heard in Mary's voice.

"Now Honey, ya know he'll be alright. He's a Sawyer. It's only fer a few days." Jonathan assured her.

Mary nodded her head and forced her tears back, and turned to Naomi and David who were waving good-bye to Samuel and Patrick.

"Naomi, David, get yer thangs. Ya better start headin' over ta school!" Mary commanded.

"All right, Ma! Come on, let's go David!" Naomi nudged David.

Patrick and Samuel's first visit was to stop off at Nielson's flour mill in Merced Falls to pick up his freight. He pulled the wagon up to the loading docks in front of the factory, and went into Harold Nielson's office on the third floor of the three-story building and knocked on his door.

"Hello Patrick. Come on in and sit down." Mr. Nielson greeted. "I have three deliveries for you; Coulterville, Chinese Camp, and Jamestown. Here is the Bill of Ladings and the note for the first half of your services, which includes the upfront costs for lodging and meals. As usual, the balance will be given to you when you return." He handed Patrick the packet of information. "Is the wagon ready to be loaded?"

"Thank you Mr. Nielson. Yep, it is waiting at the loading dock." Patrick shook his hand and took the Bill of Ladings from him.

While the foreman loaded the sacks of flour, Patrick explained to Samuel the procedure for the Bill of Ladings.

"Upon delivery, we will need to have the receiver of the merchandise sign both copies here on this line, along with my signature to confirm it was delivered. The customer receives one copy, and we are to return the other to Mr. Nielson on our way back to Merced Falls, so we could get paid." A smirky grin and a twinkle in his blue eyes stated his resolute.

After the foreman had finished loading, they signed the first part of the Bill of Lading stating his receipt of the goods.

Patrick and Samuel would now head north on Merced Falls Road towards their first destination, Coulterville, which was more than 25 miles away. But sunset was quickly approaching, so after a short distance Patrick found a place to camp.

"That seems like a good spot right over by the creek under that big oak tree." Patrick pointed out. "Why don't ya water the oxen, Sam, and I'll get a fire goin' and make us some sausage and beans."

After dinner, Patrick reviewed the itinerary for the week and details of the hauling business.

"Our first delivery will be to Coulterville. We'll stay overnight at the hotel, and push out the next day to Chinese Camp, and find a campsite outside of town. Jamestown is our final destination an' we'll spend a couple of nights there."

"Now we need to be always prepared since we are carryin' cargo. Ya never know when some outlaw will try to rob us of our goods. Ya must have yer guns ready. So keep 'em close to yer gum blanket at night." Patrick strategically placed his rifle and gun belt in his bedding.

"We'll never be carrying any money with us...just cargo.

Most bandits know that. They would have to steal the whole wagon to cart off the goods. So, more than likely, they won't bother with us." He chuckled.

"Pat. Do you suppose we can spend some time in Jamestown?" Samuel inquired hoping to pan for gold. "I'd like to try my hand out at pannin'."

"Now how did ya read my mind Sam!" Patrick grinned. "It cain't be all business ya know! Gotta enjoy yer hard labor too! Of course, we'll have time!"

Afterwards, they played a game of cards and decided to get some rest. They unrolled their gum blankets, placed their guns nearby and lay flat on their backs watching the embers of the campfire float into the night sky and fade against the glow of the stars. With the warmth of the atmosphere and the sound of the crackling fire, they soon found themselves drifting off to sleep.

AWAKE AT THE CRACK OF DAWN, they had coffee, biscuits and bacon for breakfast. They hitched the oxen to the wagon and headed north on Merced Falls Road for twelve miles and turned east on John Muir Highway for another four. Samuel played the fiddle, and they both sang along to idle the hours away on the trail.

They came to an especially small town called Granite Springs comprising of maybe three residents. Again they camped by a creek, but this night they planned to do some hunting since they were higher in elevation along the foothills.

Boomer had a strong scent for raccoon, so they set him free and they ran close by him. Not surprisingly, Boomer was barking up an old oak tree, and hissing down at him was the four legged bandit whose eyes were glaring behind his black mask permanently affixed upon his furry face.

"Good boy, Boomer!" Samuel called out.

"Alright, Sam! Why don't ya shoot him down!" Pat encouraged Samuel. "Is yer gun ready?"

"Yep." Samuel replied already positioning his rifle to his eye.

Patrick allowed Samuel to enjoy this moment. With a steady hand fixed on his target, Samuel aimed and fired! *"Bam!"* The raccoon tumbled down between the branches and to the base of the tree. Boomer stood barking at his prize until Patrick picked it up.

Tonight they would feast on raccoon stew! Samuel brought out his fiddle as Patrick skinned the raccoon and made dinner. The fur was hung over the side of the wagon to dry. They joyously sang some old-time songs and fell asleep by the campfire.

THURSDAY IS THE MOST DIFFICULT PART of the trek to Coulterville. Although only another six miles, the grade was a consistently steep climb. The four oxen struggled to pull the fully laden wagon. Walking by their side, Samuel and Boomer helped to move them along, while Patrick hollered commands and shook the reins.

They arrived at Coulterville in the late afternoon. Patrick pulled up to the general store and watered the oxen at the troughs. As Samuel tended to the packs, Patrick went inside to settle business with the owner, and returned to the wagon where he and Samuel began unloading some of the sacks of flour. Patrick also purchased provisions for the next few days on the trail.

After they had made their delivery, they headed for the livery stable, and Patrick would trade the oxen for fresh ones, and leave the wagon in the barn over night. They walked into town, checked into the hotel, and looked forward to a hot meal and a decent nights rest. Samuel tied Boomer to a post on the porch while they checked in.

"Hey Pat…welcome back! Will it be yer usual room? An' I notice you have a new partner helpin ya!" The short, bald headed clerk standing behind the front desk greeted the weary travelers.

"Hi ya, Chester. Yep, this here is my good friend, Samuel. He is the son of my employer in Snelling," replied Patrick. "We would like a room for a night, Sir, if we may?"

"You sure may! This is your key to room 204 on the second floor. Our dinner special tonight is Elsie's porterhouse steaks. And of course you can expect our usual game of poker in the saloon."

"Thank ya, friend." Patrick winked as he took hold of the keys. "How 'bout we get some grub, hey Sam?"

"I'm starved!" Samuel rubbed his stomach.

"It's a pleasure to meet you, Sir!" Tilting his slouch hat at Chester, Samuel followed behind Patrick.

They proceeded to the dining room where Elsie, a middle

aged woman dressed in a dark green printed day dress and apron, greeted them. "Well hello again, Mr. Fay. A table for you and your partner?"

"Yes, Ma'am!"

Elsie seated them in a booth. "What can I get for you gentlemen today?"

"Well, I would like the steak special, medium rare, along with a tall glass of yer finest brew!" exclaimed Patrick.

"And you young man?"

"Uh, yes Ma'am. I think I'll have the same thin' he's having except with a sarsaparilla please!"

After Elsie had taken their order, Patrick leaned forward to talk to Samuel. "Well Sam, what do ya think about the work of haulin' and deliverin' so far?"

Samuel sat back and gazed upward thinking with a grimace on his face. "I've truly enjoyed the last few days, Pat. Thank ya for considering me to come along with ya. Now I know why you love hauling freight. It's because you can travel an' see all these places an' get paid too! I appreciate Pa an' Ma havin' concern fer my future, but I am curious about what's goin' on around me outside of the farm, especially in the minin' towns."

"Well Sam, when I was your age, I thought the same way as you do. I wanted to get out an' explore. That's how I ended up in California, doin' what I like to do best. Many people were talkin' 'bout the golden treasure in these hills, so I fixed to come with my family. Fer a while, I panned an' mined, an' it was good while the gold lasted. An' that's it...it didn't last. At least not fer me. Patience is not my virtue. Prospectin' is a lot of hard work an' it pays if you can strike it rich. You'll have to find out fer yourself. The Fay family has one rule that has been passed down to ev'ry generation, *"Never be idle; if yer hands cain't be usefully employed, attend to the cultivation of yer mind'."* Patrick tapped his head while paternally advising Samuel.

Upon revealing his experience with prospecting, Samuel bombarded Patrick with all kinds of questions about the gold rush of 1849 and mining in general. Soon enough, Elsie returned with their supper as they continued their conversation. Patrick promised Samuel to go panning for gold when they arrived in Jamestown.

After wrapping his leftovers in his napkin for Boomer, Samuel untied him, and they all went to the room. It had two single beds on each side, with soft quilts and fluffy pillows, ready to bring rest to the fatigued travelers. At least Samuel could not wait to get some shut-eye. A ceramic bowl, pitcher filled with water, a bar of soap, and towels were on wash stations besides the beds, and in between them was an armoire for their clothes.

Down the hall from their rooms is a shared bath room. If they made arrangements with the hotel, they could take hot baths in the porcelain, claw-foot tub. But both men decided to do this at another time.

The outhouses were located outside; one for the gents and one for the ladies.

"Well Pat, I'm purdy darn tired. I think I'm gonna wash up, read some, and go to bed."

"Sure is somthin' that you can unwind so quickly, Sam. I'll do the same, but I'm gonna head back to the saloon for a game of poker first. Don't wait up fer me okay?!" Patrick winked and skedaddled out the door.

After he had washed up, Samuel went to bed and was

so tired that he did not hear Patrick come in around the wee hour of one o'clock.

THE RAYS OF THE SUN peeked through the window shades that Friday morning. Samuel woke up to what he thought was his Ma kissing his cheek. But when he opened his eyes, to his surprise, Boomer was licking his face ferociously trying to wake him. For a moment, he didn't know where he was until he peered over Boomer's head. Asleep in the twin bed across from him was Patrick snoring away, still dressed in his dusty trousers and suspenders and dark linen plaid shirt. At least he had the mind to take off his dirty boots before climbing on top of the soft, clean quilt.

"Oh Boomer…alright…hold on. I've gotta go too!" Crawling out of bed, Samuel put his clothes on over his long johns. He grabbed the rope which he tied around Boomers collar, left a note on the wash table to let Pat know he and Boomer would be right back, and with stealth exited the room and closed the door behind them.

When they returned, Patrick was slowly stirring. He sat up in his bed, rubbed his eyes, stretched his arms upward and took a deep breadth.

"Ooooh! Good mornin' ya two. Lord…what time is it! We better be hittin' the road soon! I'm gonna run to the outhouse too. Why don't we meet in the dining room fer breakfast, then we'll head out?"

"Mornin', Pat! Yah, Boomer and I are ready when you are. How'd ya do in poker last night?"

"Well…I'm not a millionaire yet!" Pat sarcastically remarked. "There is never a dull moment with the good ole boys. They nearly started a brawl after the game. Somethin' 'bout someone cheatin'. Sure am glad that Elsie was nearby to calm thangs down a bit. Sometimes the gentle persuasion of a woman is the remedy to defuse a sit'ation. Okay, well I've got to run an' do my business. Meet ya fer breakfast?" Patrick put on his boots and left in haste.

"Yep, I'll be there." Samuel headed to the dining room with Boomer trailing behind him.

After breakfast, they went to the livery stable to pick up the wagon and the fresh team of oxen.

Their next stop is Chinese Camp about fifteen miles away. On their way, they took the Don Pedro ferry to cross the lake. They also encountered some rolling hill tops to climb, and shallow creeks to tread. The magnificent views of the flat and widespread San Joaquin Valley could be seen from the hilltops.

It was late in the afternoon when they arrived, and Patrick pulled up to the general store. The owner, Mr. Chung, was an older gentleman, who wore a black kung fu shirt with frog buttons on the front with a high-neck collar, and light grey trousers. His long pepper colored hair, a symbol of honor in the Chinese culture, was braided into a single braid which ran from the nape of the back of his head to his waist, and resting securely on his crown was a Chinese longevity cap. He bowed to Patrick and said in his interspersed English and Chinese accent, "Come in Patrick, come in. You bring me eight sacks of flour today?"

"Good day, Mr. Chung! I sure have. Please sign this delivery receipt, and Samuel will start unloading them fer ya." Patrick replied looking forward to Mr. Chung's invitation to stay for some of his fine Chinese cooking.

"Ah, pleasure to meet you, Mr. Samuel!" Graciously bowing, he moved away from the counter. "You gentlemen join me for dinner? I will cook delicious Chinese food for you; pork chow mein, fried rice and broccoli beef stir fry. You hungry I bet! Long way from Coulterville!" Pointing his index finger at both of them, he grinned as he justified their reason to stay.

"Well, I was hopin' you'ld ask!" replied Patrick. "Ya know I love your cookin', Mr. Chung."

Samuel smiled and bowed knowing this was their cultural tradition. He has never had Chinese cuisine before. All he knew was that he was famished. So he began unloading the heavy sacks of flour as Patrick helped him.

After they had finished, the jolly little owner summoned them to go through the back door of the store which led them into the kitchen of his home.

"Come, come. You have a seat at table. I bring you food." He then brought out a bowl of hot steaming fried rice, chow mein noodles with pork and vegetables, and stir fry broccoli beef.

Samuel had never tasted such style of cooking before. Tender pieces of meat stir fried with chopped broccoli. The noodles were different from spaghetti and had a softer and thicker texture. The rice wasn't plain and bland. It was sticky and had a lot of flavor. The food tantalized his taste buds, and he could not stop himself from going for second helpings. This was far different from the meat and potatoes which he was used to.

After eating dinner, they said their farewells to Mr. Chung and brought the oxen and wagon outside of Chinese Camp to pitch their own camp. By now the sun had gone down, and it was dark. So they lit a lantern and looked for the towering rock where Patrick normally camped.

The rock was like a wall with surrounding trees. Patrick was able to hide the wagon and oxen behind it for protection and shelter. They built a small campfire, rolled out their mattresses, and fell asleep with their guns tucked under their gum blankets besides them. Having Boomer with them added a bit of comfort because of his keen sense of smell and hearing should any unwanted visitors come prowling around the camp.

The campfire had dwindled to burning embers in the late evening, and both Samuel and Patrick were sound asleep, when Boomer caught the scent of a mountain lion. He was perched on top of the rock wall and looked down on the unsuspecting sleeping campers.

Boomer quickly got up and ran to the base of the wall and began barking upwards. This woke the tired men.

"What the…!" Samuel awoke to the familiar sound of his dogs bark as he gathered himself together. "Boomer where are you!?"

"*Arghhh!*" It roared and hissed and then lunged at Boomer as he did his best to fight back.

"Mountain lion!" Trying to scare it away, Patrick grabbed his gun and shot into the sky. He did not dare to shoot at the wild animal for fear he would hit Boomer instead.

The mountain lion fled as Boomer started chasing after it.

"Boomer, no!" Samuel called out. "Boomer, come back here!"

Upon hearing Samuel, Boomer chased the cat out of the

camp and returned to Samuel with a few cuts and scrapes on his torso.

"Boomer…good boy! Good boy!" Samuel hugged his faithful friend who was breathing heavily.

"Come on. Let's get ya cleaned up." Samuel tended to Boomer's wounds and gave him an extra portion of jerky and fresh water. Samuel agreed to stay up the rest of the night while Patrick slept. He figured he could get some sleep on the trail if he needed to.

So he put more wood on the fire and sat by Boomer who cuddled up to him. But he too eventually drifted off into slumber.

SAMUEL AROSE BEFORE PATRICK on Saturday morning because he was cold and the crisp night air pained his nostrils to breathe. The fire had gone out and only a few embers were left smoldering. It was re-stoked as he threw in some kindling and wood. He wrapped himself back up in his blanket and stayed warm by the flames as Boomer snuggled next to him. Although cold, it was marvelous to be outside camping again. This reminded him of the campouts on the trail coming out to California.

The night sky was beginning to change to a pale blue, amber, then light yellow as the sun came crawling over the horizon. The sound of birds chattering and singing would burst into unison when the first rays touched the tips of the trees branches.

Finally, warm enough, Samuel took a deep breath of the mountain air, and decided to make breakfast. Again the smell of bacon, biscuits and coffee, as well as the warmth of the fire awoke Patrick with a smile.

"That was some night, wasn't it?" Patrick sat up scratching his head. "Ya never know what to expect out here in the wilderness. Thank the Lord Boomer is okay. Good boy Boomer." Patrick petted Boomer and handed him a piece of bacon.

After breakfast, they put out the camp fire, placed their bedding in the wagon, hitched the oxen, and hit the trail again. This was the day Samuel anxiously awaited because the next town to visit was Jamestown, an easy six miles away from Chinese Camp. Leaving around seven o'clock in the morning, they arrived in Jamestown by noon.

The friendly frontier town was bustling with prospectors headed to Woods Creek where gold was discovered in 1848. Some of them would go further up the road about five more miles to Sonora, and another ten more to Columbia, to find gold in the underground mines.

Patrick knew how eager Samuel was to try his hand at panning. So he pulled up to the general store and went directly inside to deal with the business owner, while Samuel watered the oxen. They unloaded the last of the sacks of flour which included the freight for the stores in the towns of Sonora and Columbia, a few miles away. They would send their own couriers to pick up their orders.

After unloading, they brought the oxen and wagon to the livery stable in town. Rustling around the wagon, Patrick fetched a canvas bag which contained two small spades, metal plates, and mason jars with lids.

"Were going to need these for pannin'!" Patrick threw the canvas bag over his shoulder. "But let's get some lunch first at the Willow Hotel and Saloon and check-in our room."

"I'll follow you!" Samuel said with excitement. "Come on Boomer...let's go!"

"Not too long ago, a mine shaft collapsed under this hotel, and 23 men died in the mine," Patrick explained walking to the Willow Hotel.

"It is believed to be haunted. But don't let that spook ya!" Patrick chuckled as he tried to scare Samuel. "No matter, they make the best barbecue ribs in town! I've gotta have some since we're here."

"Well, this ought to be good." Samuel replied with a shaky uncertainty.

After they had lunch and settled into the hotel room, Patrick, Samuel, and Boomer, with canvas bag in hand, headed for Woods Creek where all the prospectors were already panning for gold.

They were scattered everywhere along the creek, and many had earlier staked their claim. Patrick and Samuel had to do the same. So they went further upstream until they came to a shallow pool of water that collected before tumbling downstream amongst the rocks into the next level of pools.

"This is a terrific spot." Patrick surveyed the area. "Okay let me show you what to do." He removed his boots and socks and rolled up his pant legs. He rustled through the canvas bag and gathered the tools that he needed. Getting into the creek about ankle deep, he bent down and grabbed his spade and scooped a small amount of mud and placed it in the metal pan, along with some water.

"Ya simply tilt the pan side to side an' swirl the water aroun' like this. The gold will separate from the mud an' go down to the bottom because it is heavier." Patrick demonstrated as shimmering flecks appeared and settled.

"Whooohoo! Looky here Sam! These are gold flakes! Now sometimes it forms in clusters around the rocks. So you'll have to check them too!"

Samuel removed his boots and socks, grabbed his pan and spade and sank his toes into the muddy creek. After several attempts, Samuel's eyes grew large as he had the same results.

"Hallelujah! Oh Lord look at this Patrick!"

With a big grin on his face, Patrick peered into Samuel's pan with excitement. "There you have it son! I think you've got gold fever!"

Boomer began barking as he stood watching from the edge of the creek. He heard the whooping and hollering and became excited too and decided to jump in and splash around. After his swim, he went back and shook off the excess moisture from his fur, and plopped himself down under the oak tree and took a nap. The two men spent the rest of the afternoon panning. They placed their riches in their own jar of water and twisted the lids shut.

The prospectors would not have gone home had the sun not set. For many of them, they could not bare the thought of possibly missing a piece of gold in the next scoop of mud. For Samuel and Patrick, they hardly spoke a word to each other as their minds became focused on establishing a rhythm in their personal method of panning. Because of nightfall, they put their pans and spades into the canvas sack along with the jars of gold flakes and headed to the hotel for some supper, wash up and go to bed. They both agreed to wake early and spend one more day panning before returning home to Snelling.

THE MOMENT THE SHADES in the bedroom window showed a hint of morning light, they woke up, got dressed and went downstairs for breakfast.

"Well did any ghosts bother ya last night?" Patrick kidded around.

"If they did, they didn't do a good job of it! I was so tired, I slept like a baby!" Laughing, Samuel sat down in the third booth on the left side of the dining room.

But suddenly Samuel felt a lock of his hair on the back of his head being pulled. He did not think anything at first, and he thought maybe it snagged upon the high backing of the wood bench where they sat.

After the waitress delivered their breakfast, again the pull came, but stronger. "Ow!" Samuel rubbed the backside of his head.

But this time, he turned around to inspect the booth and realized he was not leaning back, so how could his hair snag. Plus the wood had a smooth finish and had no cracks for it to catch on to.

"That is the second time somethin' yanked at my hair!"

For a moment, Patrick stopped chewing and stared in shock at Samuel. "Are you serious Sam?" Patrick feeling spooked, sensed goose bumps down his spine.

"Yes!" Samuel began eating his breakfast at a faster pace. This time the tug was so strong that a couple strands lay on his shoulder. "Ow...that one hurt!" Samuel jumped to his feet, inspected the booth, then sat back down.

The waitress heard the commotion and high stepped over to their table.

"You okay?"

"I'm not sure. Somethin' keeps pulling on my hair. And it's not funny. It hurts!"

"Oh dear." Nervously looking around, she noticed the guests staring at them. "This is going to be an interesting day."

"Why? What do mean?" Patrick asked as he sat at full attention.

"Well," shifting uncomfortably, "For some reason, this particular booth you gentlemen are sitting in has had the most paranormal activity of late. A few of our guest has mentioned that their silverware levitated, or that they felt as if something kicked them in the shins. I can move you to another table if you like."

Patrick and Samuel looked at each other with fright in their eyes and simultaneously answered, "No thanks!" They wrapped up their food in their napkins and shoved it into the canvas bag, paid their bill, and ran out with Boomer running behind them.

"Ooowee...that was weird!" Samuel briskly walked towards the creek. "Do we have to stay there tonight?"

"Well...I guess not. Another hotel is down the street. We can check in after we get back," Patrick replied walking in stride.

"Yeah...let's do that."

The rest of the day went by fast as they laughed, whooped, and hollered finding small nuggets of gold between the cracks of the rocks. They maybe had another hour of sunlight when Patrick suggested, "Hey Sam…let's go back to town and cash in, and check into the other hotel."

Samuel observed his jar with the dazzling flecks and tiny golden stones. "Okay…but I think I want to keep mine for now, so I can show Pa an' Ma. Is that all right with you, Pat?"

"Oh, of course you may son!" Patrick replied. They gathered up their belongings and headed to the bank in town where Patrick cashed in his findings. They checked into the hotel down the street, had supper and went to bed early.

IT WAS MONDAY MORNING and Patrick and Samuel woke up with body aches from stooping down all day on Sunday.

"Lord, am I sore!" Patrick exclaimed while rubbing his lower back.

"Yah me too. But that was loads of fun!" Samuel replied. "Can I come with ya again on yer next delivery!?"

"You betcha Son!" Patrick gleamed. They gathered their belongings, had some breakfast, and headed to the livery stable to fetch their oxen and wagon. This time traveling back home was faster since the road was downhill most of the way, they had no cargo, and no deliveries were to be made. Instead of five days, the return took them only four.

The last day of travel on Merced Falls Road, they spent their time hunting for wild cattle and shot a heifer to bring home. They roped it and used the oxen to pull it up into the wagon bed.

They dropped off the signed Bill of Ladings to Harold Nielson at the flour mill, who in turn gave Patrick a note for the balance owed him for his hauling and delivery services.

On the same day, Thursday, they returned to Snelling and were elated when the farm came into view. They were sore, tired, and hungry for a delicious home cooked meal!

Jonathan was outside tending to the animals, when he recognized them at a distance, turning right on La Grange Road from Merced Falls Road. He remembered his conversation with Patrick at the kitchen table, and recalled the number of days it would take to make this delivery. He counted on his fingers. "Yep…nine alright," he thought to himself.

Pulling up to the barn, Patrick, Samuel, and Boomer jumped out of the wagon to greet Jonathan, who was standing with his arms crossed around his chest, and a grin on his face. He was sure glad to have them back safe.

With enthusiasm, Samuel grabbed the small jar with the gold flecks and nuggets and walked swiftly over to Jonathan. "Hey Pa! I had so much fun! Look what we brought home!" as he hugged his father and shoved the jar into his hands.

Jonathan inspected the contents in amazement and noticed the dead heifer in the back of the wagon. "Whoa, seems like ya boys did more than deliverin' flour."

"Yep. Samuel proved himself to be of valuable service for me on this trip. We had a grand time up in them hills!" Patrick remarked as he gave Jonathan a firm hand shake. "A job will be available to him with me anytime."

"Well that is mighty good to hear. But ya know he's got plenty to do around here on the farm. In fact, I'm ready to start buildin' the farmhouse next week. So both yer timin' couldn't be better!" Jonathan replied with a tinge of envy in his heart. He does not recall ever spending that much time alone with Samuel, doing father and son bonding.

"It is so good to have ya both home again. Well let's get some of this heifer cooked up an' the rest put on ice. Then we'll sit down for supper an' ya boys can tell us all about yer trip."

Mary, Sarah, Naomi, and David rushed to the cabin window and watched what was going on outside. So they came running to greet Patrick, Samuel, and Boomer. Samuel took the jar from Jonathan and passed it around to everyone to stare and gawk at.

"Ma…this is fer you! And I know where to get more too! Patrick is making several deliveries before the end of the season is out, and he already said I can go with him, and I cain't wait!" Samuel stated with a cheerful disposition.

"Oh my goodness, Samuel!" Mary gasped as she held the jar in her hand and realized that Samuel had already made plans in his mind. She didn't know whether to be upset or to be happy, and she sure did not want to say 'no' while Patrick was around, after what he has done. "Whoa…this is real gold in its purest form! Thank ya, son!"

They went into the cabin and chatted as Mary prepared a sumptuous supper and listened to Samuel. Patrick relaxed at the kitchen table with Jonathan and smoked his pipe and interjected a thing or two into Samuel's tales of grandeur. He never imagined his deliveries as grandly as Samuel described. But, he thought to himself, one day the novelty will wear off, so why not let him boast.

Patrick, nor anyone else in the family, did not realize that the novelty was not going to wear off quickly for Samuel. His heart yearned to return to the foothills to pan for gold. That was all that Samuel thought and spoke about.

8

Sarah's First Love

THE FOLLOWING SUNDAY, September 24th, Pastor McSwan would be preaching at the Snelling Courthouse. The whole family looked forward to hearing him again, and Sarah longed for another moment to be around Joshua.

Both Sarah and Mary had worked on a new rose colored day dress for Sarah to wear with a hoop skirt. Under the bodice, she wore a tight fitting corset, to make prominent her ladylike figure that she was now growing into at her sweet age of fourteen, soon to be fifteen. The satin Victorian bonnet of the same color was made to frame her face, and allow her soft brown ringlets of hair to drape over her shoulders.

After breakfast, they dressed in their 'Sunday goin' to church clothes', and the whole family climbed into the wagon. Upon arriving at the Snelling Courthouse, Pastor McSwan waved to them motioning them to come in. It had a staircase ascending from the front yard walkway to the second-story porch that led them to the double doors of the courthouse. The jailhouse was located on the first floor and was only accessible through the Marshall.

Pastor McSwan did not have a building as of yet for his nondenominational Christian church, so he rented the courthouse to conduct his services. The congregation sat in the visitors section, and he preached from the platform below the judge's desk. The facilities were never used on Sunday, so it provided an opportunity for the prisoners in jail on the first floor, to hear the Gospel of forgiveness, redemption, and salvation through Jesus Christ.

Waiting to greet the congregation at the top of the steps, Pastor McSwan smiled and waved to them.

"Welcome, Sawyer family!" Pastor politely shook their hands. "Thank the good Lord you are able to attend service today! Come on inside and find yourselves a seat and we will be starting in a little while. My family is sitting in the front row. I'm sure they would love to know you arrived."

"We are glad to be here, Pastor!" Jonathan replied as he motioned the children inside the courthouse. The girls walked in first, with Jonathan and the boys following. The McSwan family turned in their seats to observe who was coming in through the front doors. Simultaneously, both Joshua and Sarah's eyes met. Warmth flushed to her cheeks, and she thought her face must have become as rosy as her dress. After smiling at Joshua, Sarah focused on the back of her mother's hat trying not to make her intentions obvious. Mary greeted Ruth, and motioned Sarah to come frontward to do the same, and find a seat behind them.

"My goodness, how beautiful you are today, Sarah."

Ruth adored Sarah's new day dress. "You are blossoming into a fine young lady!"

"Thank you, Mrs. McSwan." Sarah bashfully curtsied. "Your words are kind." Sarah then glanced over to Joshua whose eyes were fixed upon her as if in a trance.

She walked over a few seats on the second row behind Joshua and whispered. "Hello Joshua. It's a pleasure to meet you again."

Blushing also, Joshua could not find the right words to come out of his mouth. "Huh, huh, hi Sarah. I am glad you can be here. You look real pretty today."

"Golly," Joshua thought to himself, "why did I mention that for!"

"Oh, I mean…"

Sarah interrupted before he could utter anything more and become tongue-tied.

"Thank ya, Joshua, and you are quite dapper yourself." She responded in a demure but warm gesture.

At that moment, Jonathan and the boys followed behind Naomi and Mary, motioning Sarah to scoot over a few more seats. She was seated behind and three chairs over to the left of Joshua. So she noticed his every movement as she also listened to the Pastor lead the congregation into singing hymns. Afterward he began his sermon.

Joshua sensed Sarah's gaze, which made him nervous, so he did his best to concentrate on worshipping God and listening to his father's sermon.

Pastor McSwan took a deep breath and began to preach. "Today, I am going to talk about farming." He thought himself to be wise as he spoke to a congregation comprising of 90 percent farmers. "Let me read to you from Matthew chapter 13…

Behold, a sower went forth to sow; and when he sowed, some seeds fell by the way side, and the fowls came and devoured them up. Some fell upon stony places, where they had not much earth: and forthwith they sprung up, because they had no deepness of earth. And when the sun was up, they were scorched; and because they had no root, they withered away. And some fell among thorns; and the thorns sprung up, and choked them. But other fell into good ground, and brought forth fruit, some a hundred fold, some sixty fold, some thirty fold. Who hath ears to hear, let him hear."

The pastor had Jonathan's attention…at least during the reading.

"How could Pastor have known what my crops had produced?" he thought to himself. His thoughts drifted off thinking about his first harvest, the break-even profit, and his strategy to improve the following year.

Before too long, the pastor was closing the service asking everyone to bow their heads in prayer.

"Lord, we thank you for your bountiful harvest. We pray for the seed of your Word planted in our hearts to grow and be fruitful in our lives. May you bless these good folks with your goodness, mercy, and love. In Jesus' name! Amen!"

After the prayer, he dismissed the congregation and quickly moved to the front doors of the courthouse to shake the hands of the church members who were exiting.

Ruth stood and turned around to talk to the Sawyers. "Thank you for coming to service today, and we hope you would come next week too! We will have services here through the winter until the weather permits us to have camp meetings again."

"We appreciate you inviting us to come to church Mrs. McSwan," Jonathan replied with a smile. "That was an encouragin' message meant for me."

Immediately, Mary turned to her husband with a suggestion. "Now Jonathan, what would you think about having Pastor and his family over for some supper next Sunday evenin'?"

"That's a wonderful idea!" Jonathan replied. "What do you say Mrs. McSwan? Do you think your family would be available to come over for supper next Sunday?"

"Now, you both can call me Ruth." She smiled. "I can think of no reason to decline your invitation. In fact, we would love to! Should the date not work out with Pastor, I'll be sure to send word to you to let you know. However, I do believe we have that evening open."

"Wonderful! Is three o'clock in the afternoon okay with ya, Ruth?" Mary inquired.

"That'll be fine! Thank you again!"

Upon hearing this conversation, Sarah and Joshua smiled at one another saying their good-byes. At that moment, Pastor McSwan joined them, so Ruth informed him of the plans. As the parents conversed, they dismissed the younger siblings to play outside, as the older followed slowly behind them towards the front door.

"So, I guess we'll be visiting you next Sunday." Joshua tried to initiate a conversation with Sarah and Samuel.

Samuel tried to think fast. "Hey, maybe we should take the horses out for a quick ride aroun' the farm! We'll show you the tree fort we made by the creek!"

"That sounds like fun! Will you be coming too, Sarah?"

"Of course! I could ride a horse as well as y'all!" She was

sensing an urge to start a playful challenge.

"Yah…sure ya can, kid sister." Samuel played along.

Joshua smiled at Sarah, suggesting as he glanced across the street, "Hey, you want to check what Mr. Jacobi has for sweets at the store?"

"Sure…let's go!" Samuel imagined the goodies on the counter. So they walked over posthaste.

The congenial proprietor was prepared for them behind the candy counter. "'Ello young volks! I bet choo have a sveet tooth!" He joyfully called them in his German accent. "Look vat I have he'ya…rock candy, gum balls, cherry lollipops, jaw breakers and chocolate fudge brownies."

They peered into the round glass jars on the counter filled with goodies. Suddenly, Sarah and Joshua reached simultaneously into the rock candy jar, his hand holding hers. "Here, why don't I buy this for you, Sarah," Joshua said gazing into her soft brown eyes.

Sensing the warmth of his touch, Sarah's knees became feeble. This little moment of time lasted an eternity to her as she gazed back at him.

"You don't have to do that, Joshua," she softly replied.

"Oh no…I insist!"

Joshua removed her hand from the candy jar while keeping eye contact with hers.

"Thank you."

She allowed him to hold her hand a moment longer, but pulled away as she became aware of Samuel approaching them after he purchased some sweets for his family with the money he earned from Patrick.

"Have you two decided yet?" Samuel inquired, trying to

assess what he had seen.

"Uh, yah. I'm going to get us some of this rock candy."

Joshua grabbed a handful and gave them to Mr. Jacobi along with his money.

Mr. Jacobi put the candy into two bags, thanked them, and continued his business.

They returned to the wagon where the rest of the family was waiting, and Sarah and Samuel climbed in. Slowly driving away, they all waved good-bye as Sarah and Joshua took one longer look at each other and smiled.

THE WEEK SEEMED TO PASS BY SWIFTLY since Jonathan had the whole family and the farm hands busy building the farmhouse. For Samuel and Sarah, they both had their minds occupied with other things as they did their work. Samuel had gold on his mind, and Sarah had Joshua on hers.

Sarah thought to herself, "What am I goin' to wear next Sunday?" She only had a couple of day dresses, and she had already worn the brand new dress to church. "Well, I guess the pale blue day dress will have to do." She decided.

So she washed it and hung it out to dry and borrowed her mother's finely crocheted, white lace collar and cameo as accessories to her attire. As for her straw bonnet, she added a dark blue satin ribbon around the crown.

The pastor greeted them as he did the previous Sunday. The Sawyers sat on the second row behind the McSwan family greeting one another as if they were old friends, using first names, except for Pastor McSwan. They called him Pastor, even though he actually preferred Uncle McSwan.

Pastor McSwan delivered the message with all reverence and confidence, being led by the Holy Spirit of God. He continued his discourse about farming. This time he taught the *Parable of the Wheat and the Tares* and how the enemy can plant bad seed in the field amongst the good.

Jonathan tried his best to keep himself focused on the teaching and not on his farm. Even the rest of the family had their minds preoccupied with the event of the afternoon visit from the McSwans'.

Apparently, the McSwans' were as eager, as little Rebecca kept peering back at Naomi and David and could not help but giggle. Ruth, had to on several occasions, whisper in Rebecca's ear, "Hush up." Of course, Joshua and Sarah were occupied with each other.

After service, Mary and Jonathan made sure the children stayed close by so they could quickly gather them into the wagon. Mary had much to do before the McSwans' arrived. So she confirmed the time of arrival with Ruth and immediately excused the family.

"Okay, we will see you in a few hours at our home!" Mary said with enthusiasm.

"Can I bring anything?" Ruth politely asked.

"Oh no, Ruth. I have everythang ready. Just bring your appetites!" Mary replied.

So the Sawyer family climbed into the wagon and sang hymns on the way home.

THE McSWANS' ARRIVED a little past three o'clock. After giving them a quick tour of the farm, Jonathan began barbecuing ribs, steaks, and baked potatoes on the outdoor grill. Mary had prepared baked beans, corn, and assorted fruit pies. They brought the kitchen table outdoors in front of the cabin under one of the towering oak trees. Mary dressed it with a white, finely crocheted material and a vase of sunflowers picked from her garden.

The autumn day was warm, and the fields were left with golden wheat stubble after the harvest. However, the trees provided plenty of shade. David, Naomi, and Rebecca took turns on the swing which Jonathan constructed out of rope and a scrap plank from the barn. He had also created some stilts out of the extra wood for each of the children.

While the adults were chatting, Samuel, Sarah, and Joshua discussed taking the horses out. So they asked their parents for their permission.

"Pa, Ma, Pastor, and Mrs. McSwan, may we take a quick horseback ride over to the creek? It's only about a half mile away. We won't be long." Samuel pointed in the direction they were to go.

Pastor glanced over to Jonathan and Mary. "Well, I don't mind."

"Yep, I suppose that will be all right." Jonathan placed the meats on the grill. "Please make sure to be back in an hour for dinner. Samuel you're the eldest, so you are responsible. Okay?"

"Yes Pa. I'll be careful."

Samuel turned to Joshua. "How well do ya ride?"

"Pretty good I recon, for a pastor's kid." Joshua snickered as they walked to the barn. "In fact, my father and I, before we start our meetings, will take our horses around the camp, into the towns and even into the deep woods in the mountains to invite people to come. We've actually been chased out of areas by some Indians."

Sarah's eyes grew wide with fear. "You've been chased by Injuns here in California? Weren't you afraid? Isn't that dangerous fer the two of ya alone?"

"Well, my father and I believe our lives are in God's hands. If it's our time to depart to Heaven, then we have the peace of knowing that it shall be while we are doing God's work and we will go to be with the Lord forever." Joshua explained with passion.

Sarah could only think of the dangers which Joshua would face as he and his father were out in Indian Territory.

Now that Samuel had been out on the trail, he didn't consider any of the dangerous situations Joshua mentioned. Most of the Indian's seemed friendly now and never desired to confront anyone unless they were being attacked.

"Well, I'll let you ride Jack. He's a good horse and knows his place. He loves to follow." Samuel adjusted the stirrups of the horses. "Sarah, you get Belle since she's gentle, and I'll take Fire since he's a little feisty."

After saddling the horses, Samuel led the group in a slow gallop over to the creek, Joshua was behind him, and Sarah in the rear.

Upon arriving at the tree lined creek, Samuel pulled up to a large oak and tied the horses.

They walked over to an enormous oak tree which had huge roots reaching deep into the soil and working its way over into the waters edge. Half of its branches hovered over the creek and the other over the bank. Right in the center, Samuel built a rugged fort made of scraps of wood from the barn. Small planks were nailed to the trunk of the tree to be used as steps.

The fort itself was ten feet wide by eight feet high, and had one side without a wall where one of the large branches reached over the creek. They would use this strong limb to crawl or scoot on top of till they were sitting above the water. From this branch, Samuel tied a rope which had knots every two feet that dangled into the water. Pulling up this rope to the open edge of the fort, they would swing into the chin deep stream. This little fort had been a relaxing getaway for the Sawyer children on weekends, after their hard work week on the farm was completed.

"Wow this is amazing!" Joshua remarked. "Did you build this Sam?"

"Yep I sure did, with the help of Sarah, Naomi, and David. Nobody else knows about this fort other than you and our parents. You've gotta promise not to tell anyone else. Ya promise?" Samuel said sternly.

"Yah, sure I promise. So can I come out here too?" Joshua inquired.

"Yes, as long as you check with us first. But you cain't bring anyone else okay?" Samuel repeated himself.

"Okay, I promise to God I won't." Joshua said placing his hand over his heart.

Inside the fort were four small wooden vegetable crates

used for seats and one large wood crate for a table. On top of the makeshift table are an oil lamp, a bag of marbles, a couple of books, and some opened peanut shells. In the corner is a fishing pole made of a long, thin switch attached to line and a hook.

Samuel climbed out upon the sturdy, strong branch and sat staring down into the water, thinking about the time he and Patrick were panning for gold at Wood's Creek. Joshua and Sarah each placed a crate near the edge of the open wall where the limb extended and sat watching Samuel as they talked.

"So how do you like living in Snelling, Sarah?" Joshua inquired.

"Oh I suppose it's alright. Work on the farm is hard and gets kinda lonely with only my brothers and sister to talk to. I haven't met too many people my age, until I met you." She turned her head to face him and slowly made eye contact with him. "How 'bout you?"

"Yah. The same goes with me when helping my father and mother with ministry. The camp meetings are a lot of fun, and we will meet an occasional family or two, but they all live far away. You're the closest person I've met my age too." Joshua stared into her eyes. "And I sure am glad we did, Sarah."

Blushing, Sarah held her composure as she made some suggestions. "I share the same sentiment as you. Do ya suppose yer pa an' ma will allow ya to come out to the farm an' visit on occasion? Perhaps you might tell 'em that you'ld like to help. I'm sure my pa can arrange fer ya to work on buildin' the farmhouse, or maybe ya can assist me in tending to the animals…only if ya want to of course."

"Yah…I would enjoy this, Sarah. I know my mother and

father has been hounding me to start working at the grocery store, now that I'll be sixteen soon. First, I have to finish my Bible lesson for the day, and then I can go to work." Joshua said eagerly.

"Well we'll just have to mention this idea tonight." Sarah smiled thinking about the possibilities of being with Joshua more frequently. "Speakin' of supper, we better be headin' back."

Samuel was daydreaming on the branch of the tree when Sarah called to him.

"Samuel, we should get home, don't ya think? We don't want to hold up supper. Ma an' Pa would be extremely upset!"

"Yep, okay!" Samuel yelled as he snapped out of his daze. "I'll meet ya both at the horses!"

Reaching down to grab the rope Samuel swung down to the bank and walked over to the horses.

Sarah and Joshua got up to walk towards the fort door. Unexpectedly, Joshua grabbed hold of Sarah's hand, and as she turned her head toward his, he gazed deep into her eyes, drew her close to himself, and kissed her.

She slowly opened her eyes after their lips parted and felt her body go limp. So she leaned into his arms as he spoke with gentleness to her, "Sarah Sawyer, I think we'll be seeing each other more often. Is this okay with you?"

"Oh Joshua…I'm hopin' so!" Sarah replied as warmth filled her senses and her knees weakened. Time seemed to stand still at that moment.

"I guess we better go." She unhurriedly released herself from his embrace. She took a deep breath trying to regain composure as he climbed down the tree steps and assisted her as she followed. The three of them mounted their horses and rode back to the farm.

Mary and Jonathan were bringing out the food and setting the table when Samuel, Sarah, and Joshua arrived.

"Good timin' y'all. Why don't ya go an' wash up before we eat." Mary began pouring sweet tea into the glasses. "Have your brother and sisters do the same."

The siblings washed their hands at the artesian pump and water barrel and returned to sit down. Pastor and Ruth were already seated at one end of the table sipping on sweet tea, and Jonathan and Mary sat at the other end, with Jonathan sitting at the head.

"Pastor, we would be honored if you would say grace." Jonathan insisted.

"Gladly!" Pastor replied. They joined hands as he began praying.

"Dear Lord, we do thank you for your goodness, mercy, love and provision, and for this beautiful day and this excellent bounty of food set before us. We especially are grateful for this wonderful family that you have brought into our lives and community, and do pray for your blessings upon our new friends and for this bounty of food. In Jesus' name. Amen."

So both families began passing the steaks, ribs, potatoes, barbecue beans, roasted corn, and pies. They all chattered and shared stories about their adventures of moving out to California. The children discussed school and Pastor and Ruth about the camp meetings and the places they had been.

Sarah and Joshua sat besides each other at the table not realizing they were displaying a certain chemistry between them. Both parents seemed to be aware and had an unspoken acknowledgment that their children had affection for one another. There was a sense of calm and joy mixed together, which resulted with a hint of a smile and a lifting of the brow. The body language of the parents was relaxed stating approval on both sides.

Subsequently, Joshua found the courage to ask Jonathan, after clearing his throat, "Mr. Sawyer, Sir, you have a beautiful farm and well, uh, Sir, if there is a need for some extra help… well I, uh, will be turning sixteen soon and, uh, well…I would like to let you know I am available to work."

Upon hearing his suggestion, Ruth and Pastor McSwan stared at each other with surprise as their jaws dropped. Not too long ago they were encouraging Joshua to step out on his own to find work around town.

They glanced over to Jonathan, who had taken a deep breath and leaned back into his chair, wiped his mouth with a napkin, and squeezed it on his lap. He paused for a moment staring down at his plate, thinking about Joshua's proposition.

"Lord," Jonathan thought to himself. "This is more serious than I imagined. Whoa."

He immediately contemplated the work which needed to be done on the farmhouse. "Joshua, I could use another farm hand. Yep there is plenty to do aroun' here. When would ya like to start?"

Sarah tried her best to contain herself as she stared down at her plate with a big grin.

Holding his breath, Joshua let out a sigh of relief after hearing Jonathan's answer. He too maintained his self-control trying not to appear too anxious, and not revealing his true intentions of wanting to work at the farm.

"Well Sir, I am ready to start anytime."

He then turned to his parents for their permission. "Is this okay with you, Mother and Father?"

Still caught off guard, Pastor McSwan replied to his son with stammering words. "Oh, uh, well sure, son. This is an extremely responsible thing to do! I am impressed by your motivation. You have both of our blessings!" Pastor said as he and Ruth smiled at their son.

"Okay. Well that settles that," Jonathan slapped his knee. "Why don't you plan on comin' by tomorrow in the mornin' and I'll get ya started."

All the while Jonathan knew where Joshua's request was leading. He turned to Mary who nodded in approval.

Mary grabbed the pie and joyfully scooped a portion into her plate. "More dessert anyone!?" She passed a piece over to Joshua.

Nearing six o'clock, they were all relaxing finishing dessert, when unexpectedly the ground trembled beneath them. The table and the glasses of sweet tea vibrated. But the ruckus and noise of the horses whinnying, the restlessness of the cows and oxen, and the barking of the hounds caught everyone's attention.

"What was that?" Mary blurted out, wide eyed.

Staring at the ripples of sweet tea in his glass, Jonathan analyzed the moment. "I do believe that was an earthquake." He glanced at everyone who expressed fright and anxiety on their faces. They all kept quiet and did not move a muscle for a moment, as they watched the ripples in their glasses settle down, and waited for an aftershock to occur. After a couple of minutes, the animals started to calm down.

"I think its over," Pastor McSwan smiled to set everyone at ease. "You all will have to get used to California earthquakes. They don't happen often. Sometimes the Lord has to remind us who is boss around here."

The sun was hanging low on the horizon, and the beauty of a warm golden radiance was cast upon everyone's faces and over the fields. This was a remarkable contrast to the earthquake they just experienced a moment ago. Enjoying the sunset, Mary reflected on the moment.

"Oh Pastor, and yet the good Lord demonstrates to us of how much He loves us through His orchestration of His creation."

"Amen to that, Sister!" Ruth lifted her glass of sweet tea to toast the occasion.

After the sun had settled below the horizon, Mary arose from her chair and started gathering the plates. "Please continue visitin'. I'm gonna clear the table."

Ruth also stood. "Oh please let me help you, and I will not take '*no*' for an answer."

So she also started collecting the dishware and followed Mary into the cabin and placed them into one of the two large metal tubs on top of the counter near the black iron stove.

Mary grabbed the kettle filled with warm water off the stove and poured half over the plates in the tub and the other in the second tub for rinsing. She took some soap and began washing the dishes as she handed the dish to Ruth, who rinsed, dried, and stacked them.

As they were doing this, Ruth complimented Mary about the delightful meal she and Jonathan prepared and how blessed the whole afternoon turned out. Mary returned the compliment stating her pleasure in the church service that morning and the day spent with them that afternoon.

After they had finished, they started heading for the front door, and Ruth joyfully turned to Mary. "I do believe we will be seeing each other more often than we had imagined! Daniel and I are ever grateful to you both for offering Joshua this job."

Understanding the meaning behind her statement, Mary also replied with gladness in her heart.

"I do believe you are right, Ruth, and I cain't wait to spend time with your family too! Oh, what pleasure it will be!"

So the two women cheerfully walked out to the table where their husbands were leaning back in their chairs, watching the older siblings' assist the younger ones in mounting the stilts.

"Well, Daniel, we ought to be headin' home before we lose the last ounce of sunlight." Ruth suggested.

"Yes my Dear. I agree." Pastor McSwan leaned over his seat, stood and stretched.

"This was a lovely day, a fantastic dinner and a most enjoyable visit with you folks! We truly appreciate you taking the time to do this for us." He then shook Jonathan's hand and cupped Mary's hand in his.

"Mary, my Sister, you make a mean peach pie! Not only will Joshua be around more often, but you might be visited by Ruth and I as we come begging at your doorstep for another taste of your delectable cooking!"

"Oh Pastor, the pleasure is ours! We expect y'all to visit any time!"

Ruth gathered her children, who were playing by the oak tree. After putting down the stilts, they walked over to the horse and buggy and gave their hosts a loving hug.

Joshua whispered to Sarah. "I'll see you tomorrow."

Sarah smiled back and nodded. "I cain't hardly wait."

The McSwans climbed into the buggy and headed for home.

JOSHUA ARRIVED AT THE FARM at nine o'clock the following morning. Naomi and David had already left for school, and the rest of the family and farmhands were at work on the farmhouse. He found Jonathan reviewing the plans on a table outside of the cabin.

"Hello Mr. Sawyer!" Joshua said anxiously.

"Good mornin' Josh! Ya ready to go to work?" Jonathan chuckled.

"Sure am!"

"Okay, I hope you can handle a saw 'cause I'm gonna have ya help Sam cut some of these planks." Jonathan had Joshua follow him to the farmhouse so that Samuel could instruct him.

"Now, if ya need a break fer whatever reason, come on in the kitchen and Mary will get ya somethin' to drink. Ya know where the outhouse is. Lunch is at noon fer 'bout an hour. Most of the farmhands bring their lunch or go home, but you can have a meal with us in the cabin. The day starts at eight o'clock, and we are usually done by four. Now how does five dollars a week sound to ya?" Jonathan asked.

"That's mighty fine, Sir!" Joshua responded with appreciation.

"All right, I'll have Sam show ya what to do. If ya need anything, I'll be in the cabin." So Jonathan returned to overseeing the plans.

Sarah was busy tending to the farm animals and saw Joshua and Jonathan heading towards the farmhouse. She never felt so giddy before, and her chores seemed easier and delightful knowing Joshua was nearby.

Soon enough it was lunch time and the family, including Joshua, sat down for a meal in the cabin. Mary prepared some sandwiches and lemonade for the hungry crew. They all chattered about their chores and how well Joshua was doing working with Samuel.

Afterwards, Sarah and Joshua had a little time left to talk before going back to work. So they watched the horses by the fence of the corral.

Mary, Jonathan, and Samuel watched them from the cabin window as Samuel thought out loud. "I think my kid sister is in love!"

"I think you are right Sam." Jonathan laughed at Samuel being in a giddy mood himself. "An' she beat ya to it!"

With a big grin on his face, Jonathan turned to Mary who was putting the dishes away, and he took the dish towel and flicked it at Mary's hip with a crack. "Reminds me of when we were young!"

Mary winced as she played along with Jonathan's teasing. "All right ya two…best be on yer way back to work before thangs get outta han' here!"

The rest of the week passed too quickly. On Friday, Joshua showed the Sawyer family the headline in the Merced Herald Newspaper. They read the paper together during lunch.

The headline and article read, "The Earth Quake."—"*The earth quake which took place here on Sunday last, seems to have been a general thing all over the southern part of the State. In San Francisco and Santa Cruz it was particularly severe, creating great alarm among the people and not a little damage to property. In San Francisco, there is scarcely a brick building in the city uninjured, while in Santa Cruz, says a dispatch to the Bulletin, 'there was a general tumbling down of chimneys, and those left standing were turned partially around. The losses are estimated at $10,000, but may exceed that amount.' We (the Herald) have not heard of any person having been killed though in San Francisco. At this place, it was felt by very few, and those who did feel it describe the shock as being very light, but corresponding in the main with the accounts given by the San Francisco papers.*"

"Imagine that." Sarah recollected that moment. "This happened while we were together last Sunday evenin'. That's gotta mean somethin'." They all laughed and went back to work.

NOW THAT BOTH FAMILIES KNEW Joshua was courting Sarah, they seemed more relaxed around each other during Sunday service. They visited one another often and saw Joshua practically every day.

On Monday, October 16th, almost half of the Chinese farm hands did not show up to work. Yung, the foreman, informed Jonathan that many of them had family who was on board the steamer 'Yosemite' which blew up on the Sacramento River while leaving Rio Vista the previous Friday at 6:30 in the evening. It had discharged its freight and was departing the wharf when one of her boilers burst, killing probably one hundred persons and scalding several more. Over a dozen white people, thirty Chinese men, and one Chinese woman were rescued. Most of them were blown in the river and will never be recovered.

Many of the Chinese farmhands went to Rio Vista upon hearing the news because they had family members who used the steamer daily for transportation. It would take several days to discover who was missing. Afterwards a memorial service was conducted in Rio Vista, and then private funeral arrangements were held amongst the families involved at their places of residence.

This unfortunate event had set the building project behind for about two weeks. The Sawyers would almost miss their Christmas deadline. But upon the return of the farmhands, they all worked diligently and even on the weekends to recoup the lost days and wages. They were able to meet the deadline of December 15th and the Sawyer family moved into the farmhouse in time for Christmas. The cabin was now to be used as the farmhand's quarters.

9

The First Farmhouse Christmas

CHRISTMAS IS A JOYOUS TIME for the Sawyer household as they celebrate their new home. Upstairs are three bedrooms. The master bedroom on the left side of the central staircase is spacious and has a queen size bed centered on the far wall, covered in one of Mary's handmade quilts. Next to the right of the bed is a washing station with a beautiful ceramic bowl and a matching pitcher. Besides the wash station is a chamber pot to be emptied in the outhouse, at the backyard. To the left of the bed is a small iron stove for those cold, wintery nights. To the right of the bedroom door is an armoire and dresser, and on the left of the door is a vanity table and full-length mirror. There are two large windows with wood shutters; one overlooking the front yard, and the other the back yard.

Upstairs to the right of the staircase are two bedrooms half the size of the master's. The boys share the bedroom facing the front yard, and the girls are in the bedroom facing the backyard. In each room are two single beds covered in handmade quilts and a dresser in-between the beds. In the corner of the rooms, closest to the beds, is a wash station and chamber pot. Both rooms have a large window with shutters overlooking the front and back yard and have a small iron stove sitting in the corner furthest from the beds.

In-between the master and children's bed room is a shared bathroom with a claw foot tub sitting under the window which overlooks the back yard. To the left of the tub is a towel rack, and to the right is a bucket for fetching water for the bath.

The stair case in the center of the house leads downstairs to the foyer. To the left of the foyer in the rear side of the house is a roomy country kitchen with an adjoining dining room. A large iron cooking stove is against the furthest wall, with cabinet and counter space around it. The sink has its own artesian pump and faces the backyard with a window above it.

Jonathan built an oak table to seat eight people. It fit perfectly in the dining room. It too has a window that overlooks the backyard. In-between both windows is a door leading to the back yard.

The office and study is in front of the kitchen and dining room on the left of the foyer. A dual stone fireplace graces the right side of the wall and warms both his office and the kitchen and dining room. In front of the fireplace are two winged back chairs. The wall on the left has a large window overlooking the front yard. The furthest wall is where Jonathan has his desk facing the door. Behind his desk on the wall to the right, is a book case. To the left of his desk against the wall is a secretary roll top desk and chair.

To the right of the foyer is a double-door which leads into the large family room that has an immense stone fireplace on the furthest wall. Two winged-back chairs are in front and to the left of the fireplace, and to the right is a matching couch. A rectangular table with a flower vase on top sits under the window facing the front yard, and a small serving table sits under the window facing the back yard.

A porch and overhang stretches from one side of the front of the house to the other, and has wide steps in the center which lead to the front door.

The weekend before Christmas, the family took the wagon up to Mariposa to find a Christmas tree, and brought it home to decorate and grace the new living room. Again, Mary and the children baked sugar and gingerbread cookies along with a string of cranberries and popcorn embellishing the tree. Jonathan topped it with the shining tin star he crafted the previous year. The Christmas tree gloried of its sugary delights.

Mary removed the lower branches of the Christmas tree and created a beautiful wreath with an oversized red bow. She wrapped it with a garland of cranberries and pine cones. She hung her pine-scented creation on the front door and placed pine trimmings on the fireplace mantels.

THE SAWYERS DECIDED to arrange a combination Christmas and housewarming party. They invited the McSwan family, and Patrick Fay and his wife, Ingrid. Throughout the house, the aroma of Christmas dinner, spices, and pine permeated the atmosphere.

Patrick and Ingrid arrived in the late afternoon on Christmas Eve. This was his wife's first time to meet the Sawyers, although she had heard so much about them from Patrick. He helped his wife from the buggy and grabbed the hefty basket full of jams and jellies, breads and cookies, covered with a lacy crocheted doily, and large red ribbon for the Sawyers holiday gift. They walked up the steps and knocked on the door.

Ingrid was also of Norwegian descent and had originally lived in the hills of Tennessee. She had a gentle hillbilly accent like her husband. A petite woman in her mid-forties, she wore a classic, dark plum colored day dress with a white crocheted collar which hugged close to her neck, and matching cuffs on the wrists of her dress, worn over a hoop skirt. Her hair was parted in the center and pulled back in a bun, covered by a black snood.

Patrick was surprisingly cleaned up. He wore dark wool trousers and a grey vest over an olive-green plaid shirt, and a charcoal color frock coat. He even tidied up his beard for the festive occasion.

Mary and Sarah were in the kitchen cooking when the knock came. "Someone answer the door please!" Mary hollered out to the family.

"I'll get it Ma!" Samuel, Naomi, and David ran to greet their guest at the door.

"Merry Christmas!" Patrick bellowed out with his raspy, deep voice.

"Merry Christmas!" The children returned theholiday greeting.

David hurried back into the kitchen to tell his mother and sister. "Patrick and his wife are here!" They dropped what they were doing meeting them in the foyer.

Jonathan was putting logs on the fire in the living room when they arrived.

"Pa...come an' meet Patrick's wife!" David yelled into the living room.

So Jonathan dusted off his hands and joined them in the foyer.

"Hi Patrick! And this must be Ingrid! Merry Christmas! I'm Jonathan, and this is my beloved, Mary. These are our children; Samuel, Sarah, Naomi, and David." He extended his hand to shake Ingrid's, and pointed to his family.

"I am so glad ta finally meet y'all!" Ingrid took a deep breath and cheerfully absorbed all the excitement.

"Can I take yer coats?" Mary offered as Ingrid removed her cape and Patrick his overcoat.

"Thank you!" Patrick said. "And, this is fer y'all!" He handed the bountiful basket to Jonathan.

"Ah, thank you! Well, come on in to the family room and warm yerselves by the fire. Would ya care for some eggnog or wassail?" Jonathan asked as he put the basket under the Christmas tree.

"Oh my! Wassail fer me please, to start. That ought ta warm me up!" Ingrid said sweetly.

"I'll take one of those too!" Patrick stood by the fireplace rubbing his hands over the glowing flames.

So Mary poured some hot wassail from the kettle which was on the serving table in the back of the room.

"Here ya are Patrick...Ingrid."

Mary handed them their cup of wassail in Mary's fine china, also passed down to her from her mother. Miraculously the china survived the wagon trip with barely a scratch because it was carefully packed in a crate.

"Now, if you'll excuse me fer a moment. I have to finish settin' the dinner table. Then when the McSwans' arrive we can sit down an' get to know one another more."

Being polite, Mary excused herself, so she could return to the kitchen.

"Oh please…by all means! Do what ya need to do, Mary." Patrick exclaimed.

Samuel, Naomi, and David sat down on the hand-woven carpet near the fireplace next to their father, who relaxed on the winged-back chair. Patrick sat down next to his wife on the couch and began sharing his stories about being on the trail and hauling cargo from one town to the next. He had them laughing and giggling at some of the extraordinary encounters he had with people from different places.

At this time, there was another knock and David and Naomi raced to see who could open the door first.

"Merry Christmas!" The McSwan family greeted with joy filled hearts.

"Yeah!" Naomi and David screamed as they grabbed Rebecca by the hand and rushed her into the living room to play some games by the warm fireplace.

"Merry Christmas! Come on in!" Jonathan greeted the festively attired family.

"The McSwans are here!" yelled Samuel, so they all could hear.

Mary and Sarah had finished what they were doing and came into the foyer. The McSwans removed their coats and hung them on the coat rack by the front door. Everyone flowed into the living room, and more chairs were brought in as they gathered around the fireplace chatting for awhile, and sipped on some wassail and eggnog.

Mary, Sarah, and Naomi prepared a grand Christmas dinner of turkey, scalloped potatoes, green beans, cranberry relish, hot cross buns, gravy, pecan and pumpkin pies, and Christmas cookies!

"Well I hope y'all are hungry!" Mary said over the chatter and laughter. "Let's go to the dining room and enjoy Christmas dinner!"

They followed Mary's lead and sat down at the expanded dinner table. Jonathan joined the table and chairs from the cabin to the dining table so that everyone could be seated. Pastor McSwan had the honors of blessing the home and the meal.

Afterwards, they gathered in the living room where the Sawyers brought out their instruments and played joyous Christmas carols to sing and dance to. While the families were merrying around the Christmas tree, Joshua grabbed Sarah's hand, and they quietly exited the room and went into Jonathan's office by the dual fireplace.

"Merry Christmas, Sarah!" Joshua said with delight as he handed her a small box wrapped in red paper. Sarah caressed the pretty little package and looked up at Joshua.

"Well, go ahead and open it," Joshua insisted.

Inside the box was a heart shaped locket on a gold chain with a small picture of Joshua's face fixed to one side. He had purchased the locket with the money he had earned working on the farm.

"Oh Joshua, it's beautiful!" Sarah's eyes welledup with tears.

"Here, turn around and let me put it on you." Joshua fastened the necklace about her slender neck.

She turned to face Joshua softly touching the locket on her heart. "I will never take it off."

"This is my gift to you, but I'm afraid it is not as beautiful as yours," Sarah said bashfully. "I did put a lot of love and care into it fer you."

So she handed Joshua a medium size box wrapped in red ribbon. Inside are a wool scarf, matching mittens, and socks which Sarah meticulously knitted for him.

"Sarah, this is beautiful. You made this for me?!" Joshua put on the scarf and mittens with joy.

"Yes, I did for those days when you'll be away from me at the camp meetings. I hope that they will keep ya warm and thinkin' of me." Sarah adjusted his scarf.

"Oh, I don't need these things to help me to think of you. You are always on my mind. But because they are made from your own hands, I will treasure them with my heart and wear them as often as I can." Joshua tenderly kissed Sarah.

They embraced one another and returned to the living room and joined in the laughter and the singing. This was a delightful way to end the year with those closest to them.

10

Naomi's New Friends - Bad Company

I T IS THE NEW YEAR OF 1866, Christmas break was over, and Naomi and David returned to school. David wore a wool coat and trousers, and a plaid linen shirt. Naomi wore a heavy cape over her day dress and linen petticoat. They both grabbed their lunch baskets and umbrellas and walked to school in the pouring rain.

The children were not allowed to play outdoors during their breaks because of the bad weather, so they had to find indoor games instead. Twenty students of different ages, cramped into a tiny schoolhouse, proved to be a challenge for some as they were forced to tolerate one another.

Most of the children had difficulty coping with the Edgar siblings, whose father worked in Merced Falls at the lumber mill. The two brother's names are Bert, who is thirteen, and Chad, who is eleven. Their sister's name is Elizabeth, or Lizzie for short, and she is nine years old.

It is believed their father was gone through the week for

work and returned home on the weekends. When he did return, he was not a pleasant person to be around. He took his frustrations out on his wife and children. To avoid hostilities with his family, he would frequent Snelling's local saloon, which did not help much coming home intoxicated and belligerent.

Hygiene was not on the priority list for the Edgar household. The children's clothing appeared as if they had not been washed for some time, and worn out shoes was handed down from one sibling to the next. Occasionally, an injury or bruise was evident on their dirty faces, and their hair was never brushed.

Naomi, who is now eleven years old, became aware of these things about the siblings. Most of the students were either afraid to befriend them for fear of their father and their unruly behavior, or prejudice towards them because of their social status being poor and neglected.

Mr. Cavern does his best to teach them, but most of the time the three had a terrible attitude and were continually disruptive in class. Many times he had to call the boys to the corner of the classroom and force them to wear a dunce hat. To Naomi, she thought that this correction did not help them at all, but rather made them more distressed, injured, and outraged at their classmates who would ridicule them.

Something about the Edgar siblings' rough exterior intrigued Naomi. She was not able to determine if she felt compassion for them, or, if by some strange reason, she had an attraction to them as a challenge for her to conquer.

So, one rainy afternoon during school lunch break, Naomi built up the courage to talk to the siblings who sat in a corner of the classroom. The three constantly teased and fought one another as vulgar words expelled from their mouths. Mr.

Cavern quite often had to separate them in different corners of the room, but today they had not yet gone that far.

Naomi grabbed a bag of marbles and approached them with caution. They appeared bewildered at first. Chad and Lizzie turned to Bert for some kind of signal or facial expression, which would tell them how they were to react to this uninvited person.

Bert's dirty blond hair dipped over his left eye, so he jerked his head to move his bangs to get a better glimpse of this enemy approaching. Naomi could distinguish his glaring dark pupils as he squinted. He tightened his lips and clenched his teeth. As she stood before him, he examined her trembling posture from head to toe, then fixed his gaze upon her fear filled eyes.

"What do you want?" Bert said with disgust.

At first Naomi became startled, but she took a deep breath. "I was wondering if y'all would like to play a game of marbles?"

"Heck no! Why should we want to play with you! Go away sissy girl!"

Bert's objective was to hurt her feelings and frighten the other children in the classroom. His abrasive response all the more motivated Naomi for the challenge. Suddenly, adrenaline overtook fear and she was emboldened to speak up.

"Why? Are ya afraid I'm gonna beat you? Whose the big sissy now!?"

At that time, Mr. Cavern overheard the commotion, stood from his desk, and started to reach for his ruler. To avoid confrontation with him, Bert snatched the bag of marbles out of her hands.

"Gimme that!"

He rearranged the desks to make enough room for them to

play on the floor. He selected the huge, clear blue shooter he called 'Blue Moon'. Drawing a 24 inch wide circle on the wood floor with a pencil, he placed his marble in the middle.

Naomi followed his lead, and found a place to sit down on the ground, and selected for herself the large white and green shooter she called 'Lime-aid', and positioned it in the center also.

They would use their marble to target their opponents, and to push it out of the ring. The winner is the person with the fewest shots.

The students could not believe what was happening and neither could Chad and Lizzie. They put down what they were doing and began murmuring amongst themselves.

"Hey, Naomi is challenging Bert to a match!" The classmates chattered. "Why would she want to play with him? She's brave. She's stupid. She's crazy!"

They all gathered around out of curiosity desiring to see the results of this strange encounter.

Since Naomi called the challenge, she allowed Bert to go first. So he grabbed his blue marble and centered Naomi's in the circle. He knelt down and aimed, and Blue Moon tapped the right side of Lime-aid which rolled about three inches to the left.

"One!" The Children counted together.

Next, he repositioned himself to the right of the ring and aimed. Again it hit Lime-aid on the right pushing it two inches to the left.

"Two!" the children shouted.

He aimed again, and this time it bumped Lime-aid on the left which made it roll back to the same place to the right.

"Three!" they counted.

Feeling the pressure, Bert laid stomach down on the floor, and put his chin to the ground, and positioned his aiming hand beneath his right eye. With his four knuckles down, thumb behind his curled index finger and Blue Moon resting in front of his thumbnail and on top of his index finger, he situated his marble so that Lime-aid was directly in his line of sight. Afterwards, he flicked his thumb. Blue Moon rolled with force, and made direct contact with Lime-aid. It ricocheted pass the circle.

"Four!" the students cheered.

"Try to beat that!" sneered Bert to Naomi.

"Humph!" Naomi turned her nose at him.

So she centered Bert's blue marble in the circle. Kneeling down and sitting on her feet behind her, she positioned her right hand knuckles on the ground in front of her knees to get a bird's eye view of the straight path her marble was to travel. With a flick of her thumb, Lime-aid rolled with speed and slammed into Blue Moon dead-on, positioning itself within three inches from the circle.

"One!" the classmates shouted!

If she stayed in the same place, Naomi would simply have to repeat her tactic, but with a little more power. This should cause Blue Moon to go pass the ring. So Naomi aimed and flicked her thumb, but oh! Lime-aid took a slight turn to the right and missed Bert's marble.

"Two." Her friends could not believe what happened.

She thought, maybe Blue Moon is too far away at this angle. So she repositioned herself to the right of the circle. From this vantage point, Blue Moon seemed further from the edge, but closer for Naomi to reach. So she aimed and *smack!* Lime-aid collided dead-on again, and Blue Moon went rolling pass the ring.

"Three!!" the classroom shouted and cheered!

This infuriated Bert. But at that moment, Mr. Cavern rang the bell on his desk. "Lunch time is over. Get back to your seats please!"

Bert glared at Naomi and clenched his teeth as she began gathering up the marbles. "I'll challenge you tomorrow."

"I'll be ready!" Naomi sassed with a teasing smile.

The next few days were rainy, so the game of marbles continued between Bert and Naomi. They both won and loss some matches. Bert, Chad, and Lizzie actually enjoyed the new-found, highly competitive friendship, although it would not be obvious by their mean spirited behavior towards Naomi. After they had become bored of playing marbles, Naomi challenged Lizzie to jacks.

Finally, the sun came out the following week, and the children were allowed to go outside. This is the first sunny day for several weeks since being confined indoors with their new friend. Bert's pride did not allow him to ask Naomi to play kickball with him and his siblings.

Naomi normally recreated with her brother David, and friends; Dirk, Ruby, Della, Abigail and Rebecca. She longed to run around and stretch her legs with them. Spending the past few weeks playing with Bert, Chad, and Lizzie resulted in her girlfriends becoming irritated with her. She knew she had to spend time with her old friends.

After eating their lunch, Naomi ran out with David and their friends to play tag. She saw the Edgar's kicking a ball between each other in the area they usually played.

Observing Naomi playing with her old friends, Bert thought to himself, "Gee what a traitor."

He continued to kick the ball around with Chad and Lizzie thinking all the while how much fun it would be to play a game of kickball, but they needed one more team member. He could not stand the thought anymore, so he grabbed the ball and told his brother and sister to wait while he asked Naomi to join them.

Bert has not experienced anxiety like this before, and his knees began to tremble. In fact, he had never had to ask anything of anyone, let alone a girl. So he puffed out his chest and marched over to where Naomi and her friends played.

"Hey Naomi! I need ya with us to play kick ball!"

Torn between her new relationship she was establishing with the Edgar siblings and her old friendships with her girlfriends, Naomi had to make a decision. She turned to her old friends who sneered at her.

"No Naomi! Yer playing with us. Ya cain't quit now."

She tried her best to respond to Bert as kindly as possible.

"Sorry Bert. I promised my friends I'd play with them today. Maybe tomorra'."

Bert had never been so embarrassed in his life, and the sense of rejection reeled over his emotions. It is similar to when his father came home drunk and threw everything around the house and slapped his mother. Eventually he would start slapping him and his brother and sister too, and call them horrendous names like 'good for nothings' or 'filthy brats.'

So Bert responded back to Naomi in anger, "Ah, forget it, ya traitor! I hate you! Don't ever come aroun' us again. Ya hear!"

This is something his mother would say to his father several times when they were arguing.

He took the ball and slammed it hard on the concrete and stormed off, leaving Chad and Lizzie standing in bewilderment not knowing whether to follow him or go back in the schoolhouse. Discerning Bert's anguish, they decided to dash home.

Before they did, they charged over to Naomi and cursed at her, "Yah! Traitor!" They spat on the ground and left the school grounds.

Naomi was devastated. Nobody had spoken to her in this way, nor had she ever heard anyone talk in this manner before. His words cut straight to the bone. Paralyzed and speechless, a lump formed in her throat and big alligator tears filled her eyes.

David walked up behind her and wrapped his hand around her elbow while watching Chad and Lizzie walk away.

"Naomi, are you okay? Come on. Don't you mind them. That's why they don't have many friends. I still love ya sis."

"Yah, and we do too," Ruby, Della, Abigail and Rebecca said as they crowded next to her to bring comfort.

Dirk told Mr. Cavern about the Edgar's leaving during recess. So the teacher made a note to remind himself to speak to their mother.

Naomi was not able to focus the rest of the school day, as she repeatedly dwelt on Bert's behavior towards her.

"This can't be," she thought to herself. "What did I do to him to deserve this treatment?"

Eventually, hurt turned into anger for Naomi. She was not going to stand for his lousy conduct, so she decided to look for him after school and confront him.

"I am not scared of them," thinking of her approach. Her first step was to lie to David to send him home after school in order for her to deal with Bert alone.

"David, why don't ya go on ahead without me. I'm goin' over ta one of my girlfriend's house to play, and I'll be home shortly, okay?" Naomi commanded him.

"Ah…can I tag along with ya?"

"No. This is girls stuff. I'll catch baseball with ya later, okay?"

"Oh, all right." Disgruntled, David turned and walked home.

Naomi had an idea where to find Bert as he mentioned to her about a short cut he found to school through the cemetery from their small house on the other side. He spoke of a relative, Uncle Bob Edgar, who had been buried there. Supposedly this uncle had shot one of the Snelling brothers a few years earlier in December of 1858 over a game called "Crack-loo". It consisted of tossing a half-dollar at a crack in the floor at the Snelling Saloon. The person whose 50 cent piece was closest to the crack without falling in was the winner.

Many believe his Uncle Bob shot Mr. Snelling over a dispute. His uncle was immediately hung with no judge or jury, and buried with a simple headstone in the back of the cemetery. Often times, Bert would go to his uncle's grave site and throw rocks at it after his father had roughed him up a bit. This is a story which his family became utterly ashamed of, and he thinks this is why his father is such a bad seed himself.

So Naomi went into the cemetery to locate Bob Edgar's grave site. It didn't take long to find it hidden from public view. Sitting down besides the grave marker with his head hanging low between his knees, is Bert.

As she crept up behind him, the dried leaves crunched under her boots, and he quickly looked back and jumped to his feet startled.

"What the heck are you doin' here!? I told ya not to bother me! Go away!"

He bent down to pick up one of the rocks to throw at her, but Naomi rushed in and kicked it from his hand.

The dirt on Bert's face was smeared from tears and sweat. His appearance was horrible.

"No, I'm not leavin' Bert! You cain't talk to me the way ya did! You don't own me, ya know!"

Shouting with her hands clenched besides her, Naomi reasoned with him. "I have had those friends long before you, and they'd be yers too if ya let them and ya stop acting like some bully!"

"Who needs them or you any way?! Oh go back to your silly friends and your big, cozy farm, little rich girl. We have nothin' in common, so leave me alone or else I'll…"

"Or you'll what…beat me up like your Pa does to ya! Well come on then."

Naomi threw her books down, took a wide stance, and put both her fists up. Working around the farm has made her strong, and she knew she had the ability to undertake this bully.

Naomi's comment about his father hit a hot button for Bert, and so he rushed at her to push her to the ground and punch her in the stomach. But before he could, Naomi pulled her arm back and swung at Bert's eye. He went flying backwards upon the dirt shaking his head, trying to keep it from spinning.

"Whoa," he thought to himself, "I've just got my butt whooped by a girl! My Uncle must be rollin' in his grave!"

"You get up ya coward!" Naomi yelled at Bert ready to slug him again.

"Okay…stop…I give up!" Bert said in humility not wanting to cause further embarrassment to himself. He was thankful no one had seen what happened.

"Dang, Naomi! Where did ya learn to punch like that?" Bert rubbed his eye, which began to develop into a nice shiner.

"As you said Bert, I live on a farm!" Naomi put her hands down. "Now would you stop actin' like a big baby and come to yer' senses. My choice of friends is my business, and you cain't do anythin' about it 'cause I can be jus' as tough as you," she replied snidely. "So don't ya ever talk to me that way again, ya hear? Or else I will never play with you or your brother and sister!"

Somehow Naomi sensed Bert, Chad, and Lizzie's enjoyment of her friendship and has turned the tables on him. She was now in control.

"Ya better be at school tomorra' with an explanation from yer Ma 'cause Mr. Cavern is lookin' fer y'all."

Naomi gathered up her books, turned and walked away leaving Bert still stunned on the ground. Her hand hurt to punch him in his eye, but she was not going to fess up to him. The biggest concern she had now is the fib she would tell her parents about her bruised knuckles.

THE NEXT DAY IN CLASS, Bert handed a forged letter to Mr. Cavern stating a reason for the three children returning home due to stomach aches from something they ate at lunch. By the appearance of the handwriting, the suspicious instructor discerned its forgery, but had no proof. The dark crescent shape beneath Bert's eye told a different story.

Mr. Cavern had seen Mrs. Edgar several times regarding the state of her children, but her condition did not appear any better since she was also unkempt and had bruises of her own. He was glad to have the siblings back in the classroom. At least here they had a fighting chance of making something of themselves. Somehow he concluded that another visit would not produce any change in her maternal upbringing.

As for Naomi, she lied to her parents stating that she had scraped her knuckles somehow when playing tag. Mary believed her, so she wrapped her hand with strips of clean cloth. Naomi told the same lie to Mr. Cavern.

During lunch time at school, Naomi approached Bert, Chad, and Lizzie to devise some sort of agreement.

"Ooowee! I got ya good didn't I!" Naomi teased looking at the black ring around Bert's eye.

"Humpf." Bert snorted.

He had no desire to look or speak to her realizing she is as stubborn as he is, and would do whatever she wanted to do anyway. Actually, he did not care if the other kids could see his bruised eye because it added to their fear of him. He was not about to reveal that it came from Naomi either. Naomi understood this too and did not desire to hurt his feelings or friendship.

"What are y'all doin' after school? I know ya don't want

anythang to do with my silly girl friends…but I do. So I'll spend time with them during lunch, and maybe afterschool we can go do somethin' together. How's that sound?" Naomi suggested.

"Yah…like what?" Chad asked sarcastically. "Yer such a little goody two shoes. We ain't got nothin' in common. You wouldn't be able to keep up with us bad guys anyways." Chad mocked in a rather prideful manner knowing this is how the other children thought of them.

The challenge ignited Naomi's competitive spirit. "I can do whatever y'all do, an' probably even better!" she blurted not realizing the trouble she was getting herself into.

"Oh Yah? We'll see 'bout that. All right, why don't ya meet us after school in front of the Snelling Saloon, then we'll know the stuff yer made of." Chad challenged this time.

"Okay, I will." Naomi replied with her shoulders back. She turned on her heels and went to where her brother and friends stood watching with immense curiosity.

"Are ya sure you want to be talkin' with Bert after what he said to ya yesterday?" David asked with concern.

"Oh, I'm not afraid of him, David."

Naomi realized she had to think up an excuse to send David home after school.

"Hey David, I'm gonna go over to one of my girlfriends house to visit and work on a project together, so don't wait up fer me, okay? Let Ma know and I'll get home in time to do my chores before supper."

"Yah. All right." David bought into Naomi's lie.

After school Bert, Chad, and Lizzie walked over to the Snelling Saloon across the corner from Mr. Jacobi's store.

Naomi did not want to be seen by David or her girlfriends

going into town to meet the Edgar siblings, so she hastily said good-bye to David, excused herself to the outhouse, and waited till everyone disappeared. When they all left the school grounds, she scurried into town towards Jacobi's store. The three siblings were sitting on the front porch of the Saloon, waiting for her. So she walked up to the foot of the steps where they sat.

"We didn't think you'd show up." Lizzie remarked hoping Naomi would not come. She knew how dastardly her brothers had become because of all the problems in their family.

"I'm a woman of my word." Naomi could not remember where she derived this statement and its significance in her situation. "Now what do y'all want to do?"

"Well." Chad stood to his feet on the steps of the porch and crossed his arms in front of him and stared down at Naomi. "First, ya have to prove to us that we can trust ya, an' you ain't gonna go squealin' like a baby an' tellin' on us."

Naomi shifted her weight over to her right foot as she held her books in her right arm, placing her left hand on her left hip, waiting to listen to the challenge.

"We've been kinda hungry these days 'cause our pa has not been aroun' an' our ma has no money fer food." Chad explained his family's situation as he glanced over to Bert who was staring elsewhere and not saying a word.

Chad subsequently turned to Naomi and stared her square in the eye.

"We want ya to go into Jacobi's Store and steal for us some bread and a few cans of corned beef, and afterward meet us at the cemetery by Uncle Bob's grave site."

Naomi could sense beads of sweat around her face, and down the back of her neck, and under her thick cape as her heart started pounding faster in her chest. She became so caught up in the challenge that her pride did not allow her to reason correctly knowing that this demand was illegal, and she could get herself into a heap of trouble. Somehow the words rolled out of her mouth, and something seemed to dominate her.

"Here, take my books and I'll meet ya at the grave site."

Because it was the cold and rainy season, Naomi wore her thick cape. Her day dress is also her working frock on the farm, and it had two deep pockets on both sides of her skirt.

She thought, "I can do this." All she had to do was walk around the store, put things into her pockets under her cape, and buy an apple or something small to distract Mr. Jacobi, so he wouldn't suspect anything. This is exactly what she did.

The store owner stood behind the counter, as usual, helping customers. She did her best not to draw attention to herself as she entered the building, so she swiftly tiptoed down one of the isles. She found the corned beef, and grabbed three cans and withdrew her arm into her cape and into her skirt pocket. Next she sauntered over to the bread isle and stuffed French rolls into the other pocket. The last thing she needed to do is purchase an apple as a diversion. Her heavy cape hid the groceries as well as her beads of sweat.

Naomi had been in Mr. Jacobi's store before with her brothers and sister after church service to buy some candy. She never actually spoke to him or paid for anything herself as Samuel did this for her.

Mr. Jacobi recognized Naomi, but was not able to pinpoint where he had seen her. "No matter," he thought.

"Gut aftanoon, young lady. Will dat be all for jou?" he smiled, as she showed him the apple.

"Yes sir!"

"Okay den. Dat vill be five cents please."

He put out his hand as Naomi handed him a nickel and walked immediately out the door. She rushed straight to the cemetery.

"Whew," she thought to herself experiencing relief because the harrowing event was over.

She found the Edgar siblings at the grave site as they promised. With wide eyes pleased at her accomplishment, she pulled out the food from under her cape.

"Walla! Supper is served!" Naomi said as she handed it to them.

Bert had a smirk on his face as he examined the rations, and glanced over at Naomi.

"Well, ya guys," he grinned at his brother and sister, "I think we can trust her."

Chad opened one of the cans of corned beef and used his dirty hand to scoop out a little and put some in between one of the French rolls. He took a big bite, and a look of satisfaction filled his countenance as he chewed.

"Yum! Ya did good Naomi. Here, ya want some?"

"No thanks, it's all yers."

She knew how much they needed the food more than herself. Plus she didn't have the desire to eat after what she had done.

"Oh, and here this ones on me." She handed Lizzie the apple. "Well, I gotta run 'cause I told David to tell Ma I'd be back before dark to do my chores."

Naomi wanted to get out of the cemetery and heave somewhere as suddenly she became sick to her stomach. So she grabbed her books and dismissed herself.

Too busy eating, the siblings were not aware of Naomi crouching behind the schoolhouse heaving. After recomposing, she walked home not wanting to think about what she had done.

THE NEXT FEW WEEKS in the bad company of the Edgar kids, Naomi became obsessed with the thrill of corrupt behavior. On several occasions, she found herself stealing from Jacobi's store, and even took food from her own kitchen to give to the siblings. She told her parents she did not want to go to church, claiming that she was not well because she wanted to avoid being recognized by Mr. Jacobi as the sister of Samuel and Sarah, who frequented the store after service. She began to speak like the Edgar's, using foul language, and became less interested in her schoolwork on account that she spent her homework time with them.

Mr. Cavern had discerned the immediate change in Naomi's grades and attitude. He noticed she had not been going straight home with her brother. So one day when all the students left after school, he closed the front doors as usual, but he quietly stayed inside the schoolhouse to investigate Naomi's conduct from the classroom window.

Not surprisingly, he witnessed her sending David away,

as she entered the outhouse afterwards. He waited until she came out and walked towards the cemetery before he followed her. Hiding behind some trees, he continued to follow her as she headed to the back where the Edgar siblings were waiting.

At first they began talking, proceeded by name calling, and throwing rocks at the head stones and defacing the trees. This is all he needed to witness, so he returned to the school and made plans to visit Mr. and Mrs. Sawyer the following day after Naomi sent David home.

THE INTENTION TO VISIT THE SAWYERS was cancelled the next day. Both the Edgar and the Sawyer children were absent. He could not help but wonder what had happened to them. Now he had to wait to receive a note from the parents explaining their absence.

Before school was over, Mr. and Mrs. Sawyer pulled up in their buggy. They waited until all the students exited before entering to talk to the instructor.

"Hello Mr. Cavern." Mary greeted rather somberly. "Can we take a moment of yer time? This is Jonathan, my husband."

"Yes of course. It is my pleasure to meet you, Mr. Sawyer, and to see you again Mrs. Sawyer. Please have a seat."

Mr. Cavern shook Jonathan's hand and positioned two chairs in front of his desk. "Naomi and David were absent today. Does this meeting have anything to do with this?"

"Yes, unfortunately." Jonathan replied, leaning back in his seat with a frown on his face.

"A terrible incident happened which we are rather ashamed to discuss. Apparently, Naomi had been caught stealing from Jacobi's store. We were visited yesterday in the late afternoon by Marshall Warner informing us that he had our daughter at the courthouse, awaiting our arrival to claim her. He informed us of their reason for restraining her. As a minor, they could not hold her in custody, and as her parents, we are held liable for her actions." Jonathan humbly reported.

Mary continued, "Well, Marshall Warner explained to us that Mr. Jacobi would be willin' not to press any charges as long as we paid fer the cost of the stolen items. He further suggested that we reprimand Naomi in a manner suitable to us…knowing our good citizenship status in our town. So this is what we did. We picked her up at the courthouse, paid our fine an' settled with Mr. Jacobi, an' have brought her home where she is to be grounded from school."

Mary shifted in her seat and leaned forward.

"Naomi told us everythang an' how she had been involved with the Edgar's an' that they dared her to do these horrible acts. After pickin' up Naomi, we made a visit to the Edgar home an' spoke to their parents. We told them that we would not mention to the Marshall their involvement as long as they reprimand their own children an' kept them away from our daughter," Mary clarified.

"We don't know what this'll do for yer school. As fer us, we have decided to ground Naomi fer the rest of the school year, an' I will have to teach her fer now. The matter that concerns us is David's attendance. This is why we are here to talk to ya.

We need to know how Naomi became involved with these children, an' whether or not David should exercise caution when attendin' school." Mary looked Mr. Cavern directly in the eyes with enormous concern.

Shaking his head side to side, Mr. Cavern leaned forward in his chair. "I am so sorry to hear this news, Mr. and Mrs. Sawyer. I do want to make it clear I had not been aware either, of the depth of Naomi's relationship with the Edgar siblings. A few weeks ago during the rains, Naomi attempted to become friends with them. I actually thought it a kind gesture on Naomi's part to try to include these children socially with the other students…or at least with herself to start. When it was sunny again, it appeared everything went back to normal, since the Edgar's played by themselves and Naomi returned to her friends."

He shifted his body forward on his chair. "But this week I became aware of Naomi's grades dropping and that she was delinquent in her homework and projects. I also noticed Naomi was not going straight home with David after school. So yesterday, I did a little investigating myself and followed Naomi. As I suspected, she was meeting the Edgar children in the cemetery. I planned on visiting you this afternoon to discuss this matter, but it seems the Lord had a different plan."

Mary proceeded trying to remain calm. "Naomi informed me that she had been workin' on a project with one of her friends after school, an' she would be home before supper time, an' I believed her! I also thought I was losin' my mind because I seemed to be missin' food in my pantry! Do you know what you are gonna do about this sit'ation, Sir?"

"Well, Mr. and Mrs. Sawyer, I believe the proper measure

would be to expel the Edgar children for their bad behavior and this terrible ordeal. This is serious indeed. Trust me this is not the first incident I have had with them in this classroom. This ordeal draws the line. I will make the effort to visit their family today. I do understand you have to do what is necessary to correct your daughter, and I would gladly provide her homework, so she may finish the year with you. Will this solution help you in making your decision for David?"

"Yes indeed, Sir!" Jonathan agreed and stood with a sigh of relief as he extended his hand to Mr. Cavern. "We will have David back in school tomorra'. Well, we better not take too much more of yer time. We have a young lady that we need to spend our time with. Thank ya fer understandin' our dilemma."

Jonathan and Mary shook Mr. Caverns hand and returned to the farm with some relief, yet troubled with what lies ahead for them

11

David's Calling

JONATHAN AND MARY had become so preoccupied with planting the new crop and managing the farm hands, that they lost track of the events happening in the lives of their children. All the while Naomi found herself in trouble with the Edgar siblings, Samuel had been on several trips with Patrick Fay hauling firewood to businesses and households from Forlorn Hope to Mariposa. At this time, Samuel brought his horse, Fire, with him so he could venture out on his own while Patrick dealt with his customers and visited the saloons for a game of poker. Samuel panned for gold all along the small creeks in Hornitos, Aqua Fria, Mariposa and Coulterville and had been gone with Patrick for several weeks at a time from January through April, so Joshua took on his slack of the work on the farm.

For Sarah and Joshua, lunch breaks, and an hour before he returned home, were spent together. They both had fallen in love, and even began to discuss marriage.

David had to learn to stand on his own two feet and not depend on Naomi's care and protection, since she had been grounded for her misbehavior. He was ten years old, wiser, and ready to start finding an identity.

After the episode with Naomi and the Edgar children, Naomi's girlfriends pretty much kept to themselves. David, on occasion, would play with Dirk, but even he seemed disinterested in their friendship. He couldn't help but think he had been shunned because of the incident between his sister and the Edgars.

With Naomi grounded for misbehavior, Samuel gone most of the time, and Jonathan and Mary busy with the planting season, only Sarah and David would attend church together for several weeks.

David found solace in reading books, and his favorite book of all was the Bible. Attending services and listening to Pastor McSwan talk about the love which God has for those who believe in Him, had made David feel loved. Due to the family's circumstances, David felt detached and maybe even forgotten. He found his outlet in studying God's Word, listening to Pastor McSwan preach, singing praises in church, and having quiet times in prayer.

IT WAS MID APRIL when Pastor McSwan informed the congregation that services were no longer to continue in the courthouse starting the month of May because he and his family will be on the trail setting up camp meetings around the Sierra Mountain foothill counties through July. They would return to Merced County in August and early September, so he invited the church members to attend those meetings when they returned.

Both Sarah and Joshua were not looking forward to this time for this meant being separated for three months. Sarah is much needed on the farm and is not able to travel with the McSwans to the distant locations. The meetings to be held at the neighboring towns in Merced County are about the only ones she can attend and will not take place until the later part of their schedule in August and September. The three-month separation shall test their love for one another.

For David, the camp meetings are an opportunity in which he desired to participate. School would be out in two more weeks, and if Pastor McSwan and his parents agreed, then perhaps he can serve God by helping with the camp meetings during the summer. So, when the congregation dispersed, David approached Pastor McSwan after the service to discuss this possibility.

"Hello Pastor. Sharin' the Gospel of Jesus Christ in Jerusalem, Judea, Samaria an' even to the ends of the earth must be very exciting. I can see why it is on yer heart to have camp meetins' to bring the Good News to towns outside of Merced County!" David's eyes glowed as he spoke to Pastor McSwan, who was listening while picking up his notes from the judges desk.

Pastor McSwan paused for a moment looking at David, realizing this young man genuinely heard the message spoken in service.

"Oh, why thank you David. I am pleased to hear you understood the connection of the message to the purpose of the camp meetings. This is extremely observant of you. Even some of the adults in the congregation do not have the wisdom and understanding as you have." He complimented David.

Smiling in his demure and almost grownup way, David asked, "Pastor, is it possible for me to go along with you an' yer family to serve the Lord at the camp meetins' this year? I believe God is leading me to do this. I enjoy readin' the Bible, an' I can help out in whatever way you desire."

At that moment, something tugged at Pastor McSwan's heart. It is as if God was prompting him and confirming that this is His genuine calling upon David's life to minister the Gospel, even at his early age of ten years old.

"Well David, is this what you truly sense the Holy Spirit is asking you to do? You must be aware it is not an easy path to take. The camp meetings are indeed a wonderful blessing, but it is a lot of work. I would be grateful to have you come with us and help in the ministry, after of course, we receive approval from your parents." He encouraged him with all sincerity.

"Pastor…I love the Lord with my whole heart an' I desire to serve Him. I sense God's desire to use me at the camp meetins'. I am willing to work real hard for ya."

"Okay. I believe you David. Why don't we pray together and let us make your request known to God, and ask for His hand of guidance. All right?"

So Pastor McSwan and David held hands, and he prayed. "Dear Heavenly Father. I present to you your son, David, and his desire to serve you, Lord, at the camp meetings. If this is your will, Lord, then we ask for your direction, and that you would open the doors needed to allow this to happen. We ask this in Jesus name. Amen."

"Amen!" David's heart leaped with joy.

"Well, I believe you should discuss it with your parents first David. If they approve, then I will gladly have them over to our house to talk about the plans. Do we have an agreement?"

"We do, Pastor McSwan! I'll speak to them this week." David was very eager as he shook the pastor's hand. "And maybe we will see you next Sunday."

"Okay, we'll plan on it!" Pastor replied with a big smile on his face.

So David joined Sarah who stood with Joshua at the front door of the courtroom. Joshua walked Sarah and David back home to the farm as David shared with them the conversation he had with Pastor McSwan.

Joshua was happy for David, but yet he had hoped Sarah would go, as well. He is aware that this is impossible. After Joshua had brought them home, he returned to his house to spend time with his family.

Sarah also envied David for having the opportunity to minister at the camp meetings. She also realized it would be futile to request this of her parents.

Entering the farmhouse she advised David. "If I were you David, I would share this news with Ma and Pa during dinner time when they had a chance to relax some. I'll try to support you too, if they ask. Okay?"

"Thanks, Sarah. Yah, I'll do as you say." David listened intently to his older sister and was appreciative of her counsel.

At the dinner table that evening, Jonathan and Mary asked Sarah and David about church and the message that Pastor

McSwan delivered. This was the open door which David had waited for.

"The sermon today truly touched my heart, Ma an' Pa," David spoke up. "It was about how Jesus asked his disciples to bring the good news to everyone who lived in Jerusalem, Judea, Samaria, an' finally to the ends of the earth. Pastor also mentioned bringing the Gospel to Merced County, Mariposa County, Tuolumne County, an' even to Calaveras County. Pastor said many people have flocked to these areas because of the gold rush an' they desperately needed to hear the Gospel…the true gold! He mentioned this would be the last month to have services at the courthouse, fer they will be startin' up the camp meetins' again in counties outside of ours all the way through July. They'll return to Merced County in August an' have camp meetins' here."

For a moment, David paused and put his utensils down and looked at Sarah, then at Mary, and finally fixed his gaze on Jonathan. "Pa, I asked Pastor McSwan if I could go with them to serve the Lord. I truly believe God wants me to do this. Pastor loved the idea an' said he would be grateful if I did. The final decision is yours to make, Pa an' Ma. I hope you will allow me to do this. May I, Pa an' Ma?"

Mary looked at Jonathan, who was counting in his head. "This would be three months you will be gone David. This is a long time, an' you are only ten years old. Allow me an' your Ma time to talk an' pray about it, son, an' I can let you know our answer in a couple of days. Okay?" Jonathan tried not to disappoint David.

THE NEXT FEW DAYS while David was in school, Jonathan and Mary met in his office and had a lengthy discussion about David's request.

"What am I suppose to think, Jonathan?" Mary paced in front of the fireplace. "David is too young to be away this long. I trust the McSwans to watch after him, but ya know they will have their hands full overseein' the details of the camp meetins'. It would be too difficult to do this an' keep an eye on our son, no matter how good a boy he is. One day, I know he is destined to be a preacher, so I don't wanna discourage him. This would be a wonderful experience fer him. This must be God's will fer David, but why so soon? What should we do Jonathan?"

"Oh Mary…Mary!" Jonathan frustrated with uncertainty, ran his fingers through his receding hairline. "There has been so much drama in our household of late. Samuel is gone most of the time pannin' fer gold, Sarah is in love, Naomi is grounded, an' now David wants to go away fer three months to evangelize! What's next!?"

Jonathan leaned back on his chair and stared out the window praying quietly to himself. He began thinking about the camp meeting they attended the previous year and how wonderful the experience had been for the children. They all accepted Jesus as their Lord and Savior at this event.

This thought led to a possible solution. "Now, here's an idea Mary. What if we allow David to help Pastor McSwan at the camp meetins' in Merced County when they return in

August? This way he can be close enough to home should he need us. Also, this will give him time to ease into the ministry an' experience it first. Plus he'll be away for only one month. Perhaps, in a couple of years, when he is twelve, he can go with them on the three-month journey. What do ya think about this?"

"This is a brilliant compromise, Jonathan! One month away seems reasonable for his age." Mary agreed and walked over to her husband and embraced him.

So in the afternoon when David returned home from school, Mary and Jonathan explained to him their plan. Although it had not been the entire summer he had hoped for, David understood his parents concern and found contentment with their decision to allow him to be gone for one month. He planned to hold them to their promise that he would be allowed to go with the McSwans for three months when he turned twelve years old.

So, the Sawyers discussed the camp meeting plans the following Sunday during dinner at the McSwan's home. They were all pleased with the idea and grateful for God's calling in David's life.

PASTOR MCSWAN AND HIS FAMILY scheduled camp meetings in Calaveras County (the furthest away) in May, Tuolumne County in June, and Mariposa County in July. They would reach so many people with the Gospel message held in various places.

The parchment invitation headline read, "Camp Meeting Under the Brush Arbors!"

Several arbors were to be built around the cleared areas to provide shade for the congregation and also for the pulpit where Pastor McSwan preached.

Posting flyers in downtown store front windows, placing notices in town newspapers, and visiting folk in remote locations of these counties to invite them to the camp meetings is difficult and time consuming tasks. But it paid off for many had been saved and blessed to listen to the Gospel message of eternal hope with God in heaven.

The sermon proved timely for people who came for the gold rush. Countless pioneers had become discouraged because they did not "strike it rich", so they began living riotous lifestyles filled with debauchery, sickness, and death due to typhoid fever and cholera.

The camp meetings provided the opportunity for hundreds, and even thousands of people to gather to experience recreation and spiritual renewal. Some found their marital partners at these meetings, like Joshua and Sarah hoped to do. Many enjoyed the "physical exercise" of praising God through worship songs and dancing about in the Spirit as King David did in the Bible.

Not only did they reach all the gold prospectors, but they also reached some of the Indians living in the foothill areas, as well as the many Chinese immigrants working for the Pacific Railroad laying down track through the Sierra Mountains.

BY THE TIME THE MCSWAN FAMILY RETURNED to Merced County, they began to sense exhaustion and the toll upon their own lives. However, the satisfaction of knowing the multitudes that had been saved from hearing the Gospel, far outweighed their sufferings for Christ.

Camp meetings are to be held in Merced County during the last leg of their journey in the months of August and early September. Their first is to be at Merced Falls in mid August.

The Sawyer family planned on attending the camp meetings in Merced County. They helped to serve the people by playing music and hymns for the services. They would allow David to remain with the McSwans while they returned to the farm after the weekend ended. Elated to finally be over the grounding period and back out into society, Naomi welcomed the meetings, so she could be in the company of her friends again.

David's service is certainly appreciated by the already exhausted McSwan family. He assisted in posting flyers around the towns, setting up the brush arbor area for the camp meetings, and helping Ruth and Rebecca as they ministered to the children in their own Bible studies.

The second camp meeting in Merced County is located in Forlorn Hope at the end of August, and the third is held in La Grange at Branche's Ferry in early September. This is the same event that the Sawyers attended the previous year.

12

Troubled Times

SARAH WAS RELIEVED to have Joshua back in the area to be near him, at least on the weekends when they had the camp meetings. The time they did spend with one another, she found him literally collapsing on her lap and falling asleep from exhaustion. Although he was exhausted, he never complained, but rather spoke highly of how God had been moving in the lives of the people at these camp meetings. She began to grow concerned for Joshua because he had lost a tremendous amount of weight and the color of his skin seemed to be pale and clammy.

It was during the last camp meeting in La Grange, on Saturday evening that Joshua came to the Sawyer campsite to visit Sarah when he collapsed in her arms. His head felt warm, and his body lay limp and in a cold sweat. Aware of the five-month journey soon to end, Joshua never complained to his parents of his bout with diarrhea and headaches that occurred within the final thirty days.

"Joshua…Josh…wake up…wake up!" Sarah screamed as she held him in her lap. "Pa, Ma, come quickly! Pa, Ma!" Trembling and rocking Joshua's lifeless body, Sarah sobbed uncontrollably trying to revive him.

Jonathan and Mary were astonished as Sarah sat on the ground cradling Joshua, so they ran immediately to her side. Spreading a blanket next to them, Jonathan picked him up and laid him upon it. After Mary had placed a wet towel over his temple and a cup of water to his pale lips to force him to drink, Jonathan tried to shake Joshua's body trying to kindle a response. Sarah held Joshua's hand as she wept uncontrollably.

"Continue to try to wake Joshua and hold this compress to his head, Mary, while I run to find Doctor Cassidy and Pastor McSwan." Expeditiously, Jonathan ran to their camps and informed them of Joshua's condition. Pastor McSwan was meticulous for having a doctor at the camp meetings should his services ever be required. He never thought his own son would be the one to need attention.

Doctor Cassidy diagnosed Joshua as having cholera and extreme dehydration. August and September are the sweltering months of the year, and it only intensified his poor condition. The whites of his eyes were visible as his pupils rolled back. The Doctor did his best to administer water to rehydrate him. Pastor McSwan, Ruth, Mary, Jonathan, and Sarah encircled Joshua and prayed.

After several minutes of cooling him down with wet towels and trying to get him to drink, Joshua slipped away peacefully and went home to be with the Lord. The families grieved for what seemed like an eternity.

Afterwards, Doctor Cassidy stood and suggested he fetch

his wagon to bring Joshua's body to his office in town where he can prepare him for burial. Both Sarah and Ruth planned to accompany the Doctor, while Rebecca stayed with Mary. The rest of the Sawyer family remained to help Pastor McSwan complete the last day of camp.

The three hour ride to Snelling became unbearable for Ruth and Sarah as they held each other and wept in back of the wagon where Joshua's body lay covered. All Sarah could contemplate was what Joshua had told her when their family came over for supper for the first time at the farm the previous year.

Joshua spoke of his resolve regarding dangers he and his father encountered at the camp meetings. He passionately stated, "Well, Pa and I believe our lives are in God's hands. If it's our time to go, then we have the peace of knowing that it will be while we are doing God's work and we will go to be with the Lord forever." His words continued to resound through Sarah's mind over and over, trying to convince herself that this was God's plan for Joshua.

After laying Joshua's body on his examining table, Doctor Cassidy left the room, so the ladies had time to express their farewells. Sarah went first as she mourned and told Joshua how much she loved him and promised to think of him always. After several minutes, Sarah summoned Ruth.

Sitting in the doctor's waiting room, Sarah immediately ascertained Ruth's excruciating pain and sensed her agonizing sorrow. Ruth embraced her son and lamented for some time before she emerged from the examination room. She placed her arms around Sarah's shoulder, and they walked to her home where Sarah stayed the night and would be retrieved by her parents the following Sunday evening on their return from La Grange.

Sarah caressed the pillow on Joshua's bed as she viewed the articles on top of his dresser in his bedroom. Neatly arranged was her tin type picture, a wooden cross that he had whittled at a camp meeting, a couple of Indian arrowheads, and a pile of parchment flyers of past camp meetings he kept as souvenirs. She lay weeping on his bed, cradling his pillow, exhausting every ounce of energy she had left causing her to fall into slumber until her parents arrived the next evening.

THE FAMILIES DID THEIR BEST to suppress the news of Joshua's death to avoid alarm for the many campers. But to no avail, the report circulated and the people lamented for the McSwan family, so they lifted them up in prayer and sympathized over their loss.

The Sunday morning service was somber as Pastor McSwan closed the session trying to encourage the congregation, as well as himself, to have peace knowing Joshua passed away doing what he loved best, serving his Lord and Savior Jesus Christ.

"Joshua departed in the arms of those who dearly love him, and now he is in the embrace of the One who loves him most… the Heavenly Father." Pastor McSwan announced with deep grief and tremble in his voice to the weeping crowd.

He demonstrated the comfort and peace only Jesus Christ can offer to Christians who have lost someone they love, knowing his son was at a good place, home with the Lord where one day they will meet again. Joshua's death and hope of eternal life magnified the message of salvation to a lost and dying world. Of all the camp meetings, this event had the largest impact, as many people accepted Jesus Christ as their Lord and Savior and understood God's promised of redemption.

The ride back home was still and sorrowful for both families. They gathered once more for prayer and weeping at the McSwan's house Sunday evening. Numb from the last 24 hours of trauma, Sarah became weak and lifeless. Jonathan had to carry her back to the wagon as Mary held her.

Upon arriving at the farm, Jonathan carried his daughter and brought her to her bedroom. Mary helped Sarah to change into her nightgown and tucked her in bed where she remained the next few days. Mary did her best to get her to eat, but she did not have the appetite. Finally, by Wednesday, she tried to recompose herself by eating a small portion to gain enough energy to attend Joshua's funeral that morning.

The outpouring of love for the McSwans' came from the town and the church members as they provided meals for the grieving family every day for two weeks. Flowers, cards, and letters with financial help were delivered to support and sustain them, and to cover the cost of the funeral.

Joshua's memorial was held at the Snelling cemetery. Pastor McSwan did his best to contain himself as he conducted the service. He read Psalm 23 and then reflected upon Joshua's faithfulness to the Lord and to his family as a loyal servant and only beloved son.

Ruth and Rebecca sat next to Joshua's coffin. They had cried so much the last few days that no more tears were left to cry, until the end when his casket was being lowered into the ground. This is it. No longer will they see Joshua, until they meet again in heaven. Ruth shuttered in sorrow and tears began to flow, and Sarah fell to her knees and sobbed on her mother's shoulders. The families and friends placed flowers over his final resting place and somberly returned to the McSwans' home to offer their condolences.

For Sarah, it would be a long while after the funeral before she interacted with the McSwans. It was too difficult for her to bear to attend church and have fellowship with his family. Eventually, she became angry at God for taking him away from her and could not bring herself to giving God any thanks after what happened. Jonathan, Mary, and especially David, did their best to comfort her, but she had no desire to partake in church or with God.

Jonathan consoled his daughter, "Sarah, Darlin', we love Joshua an' considered him a part of our family. God must have loved him more than we do, an' probably has plans for him in Heaven. He loved God so much that he had peace knowing there was the possibility of losing his own life for the sake of spreading the Gospel. The ultimate reward that Joshua could have ever wanted was to be eternally with the Father in the most beautiful place of all, Heaven! This is where those who love Jesus shall one day reside, with Him forever. Don't lose your faith, daughter, for you will see him again."

They sat on the rattan couch at the front porch of the farmhouse. Jonathan hoped to bring Sarah comfort by explaining Joshua's heart and position regarding his calling to serve God.

"But, I needed him Papa! I needed him!" Sarah sobbed.

"How can God do this?! It's not fair!"

"He can do this because He is the Sovereign God an' he is all knowing an' has His reasons. We need to trust Him. His Word tells us in Jeremiah 29:11-14, '*For I know the thoughts that I think toward you, says the LORD, thoughts of peace and not of evil, to give you a future and a hope. Then you will call upon Me and go and pray to Me, and I will listen to you. And you will seek Me and find Me, when you search for Me with all your heart. I will be found by you, says the LORD.*'" Jonathan placed his arms around Sarah's shoulders.

"He knows what is best for us. One day he shall reveal this to you, Sarah."

Somehow this answer still did not settle with her, for at this moment, she did not desire to know God's reason for taking Joshua so early in life.

Day by day her heart grew colder and more distant. She would dismiss herself anytime God was mentioned. The family members were careful not to push her and allow time to heal her broken spirit and for God to reveal himself to her.

TWO WEEKS HAD PASSED before Rebecca returned to school. She seemed so despondent, and she did her best to concentrate on Mr. Cavern's teaching. At lunch time, she found a quiet, shady spot under a tree. Ruby, Della, Abigail, and David would sit by her to encourage and comfort her.

Rebecca finally began to smile again after eight dreadful weeks of experiencing roller coaster emotions.

David walked Rebecca home from school everyday and spent time reading from the Bible to the family before he returned to the farm. Having David around helped the McSwans' cope with their grief. He grew all the more closer to them as he did his best to comfort and encourage them.

An occasional slip of speech occurred when Pastor McSwan would accidentally call David, 'Joshua'. After realizing what he had said, he broke down in tears.

"Pastor an' Mrs. McSwan, it's me David. I brought Rebecca home!" David hollered through the screen door, and opened it to allow Rebecca and himself in the house.

"Hello children, come inside." Pastor McSwan came out of the kitchen with Ruth and gave them a hug.

"Is there anythang I can do fer ya today?" David offered his service.

"Oh David, you're such a gracious young man," Ruth commented. "Would you like a glass of lemonade?"

"Yes Ma'am, if it's not too much trouble," David replied. "I know--may I read to you both from the Bible? That is if you wouldn't mind me spendin' some time with y'all."

"Well, this is a wonderful idea David." Pastor McSwan walked over to David and patted him on his back.

"Indeed! Why don't the three of you sit out on the porch and I'll bring the lemonade." Ruth returned to the kitchen to prepare some refreshments.

"Come David. Let's do as Misses Ruth tells us." Trying to hide his pain, Pastor McSwan had a slight grin and winked at David.

So they went out on the front porch. He sat on his rocking chair, and David and Rebecca on the swinging bench with their Bible and school books in between them. Ruth brought the pitcher of lemonade and four glasses and placed them on the white rattan table in front of the chairs. After pouring each of them a glass, she sat in her rocking chair next to her husband.

"How 'bout I read from the book of John, Pastor?" David suggested.

"That is perfect for us to hear, David." Apostle John brought to attention the essence and awesome power of God. Pastor agreed this would be very comforting to his soul.

So David read. *"In the beginning was the Word, and the Word was with God, and the Word was God. The same was in the beginning with God. All things were made by him; and without him was not any thing made that was made. In him was life; and the life was the light of men. And the light shineth in darkness; and the darkness comprehended it not..."*

David read a chapter a day to the family everyday after school, up through Christmas break, and they looked forward to his daily visit and reading. Pastor McSwan poured himself into David and taught him the Scriptures and answered his questions. His visits helped to get their minds back on God and to heal their hurting hearts.

SUNDAY SERVICES RESUMED at the Snelling courthouse one month later in October. David went to church early to help prepare for service. Preaching deemed emotionally difficult for Pastor McSwan, but he proved himself to be faithful to God through his perseverance, despite the pain. He epitomized the steadfast faith of the apostles. Even when faced with complicated circumstances, he did not give up. David grew stronger in his faith and in the knowledge of the Lord because of what had happened and by learning from the godly example that Pastor McSwan provided.

CHRISTMAS HAD MANY SOMBER MOMENTS at the Sawyer farmhouse as they continued to mourn the death of Joshua. The tree had shown brightly but dulled in comparison to the joy the prior year. They exchanged gifts and had Christmas dinner and sang Christmas carols together. Not too long after the expected holiday traditions began, Sarah dismissed herself to her room where she cried to sleep as she had done the months prior.

Samuel held off until after the New Year in 1867, and after his eighteenth birthday in January, to tell his parents that he planned to move to Jamestown where he would be closer to the gold mines and creeks. Before he sprang this difficult news on them, he wanted the dust to settle first. He had saved quite a bit of money he earned panning and working for Patrick for this reason.

The end of January is when Samuel informed them of his decision to leave home. He asked to speak with them privately in the office. They each pulled up a chair besides the fireplace. Both Jonathan and Mary braced themselves for they had anticipated this moment to occur one day.

"Pa, Ma, I've decided the time has come fer me to get out on my own. Last year I worked hard an' saved enough money to purchase a wall tent so I could camp out next to the creek in Jamestown. I figure I might make a livin' from prospectin' fer gold. If this doesn't work, I can always find employment at the railroad. Plus, I will still continue to help Patrick out with haulin' freight." Samuel paused to receive a response from his parents.

Suddenly, Mary's throat tightened, and a knot welled up in the pit of her stomach. She found herself at a loss for words. She looked over to Jonathan who seemed to be experiencing the same, but held his composure better than she did.

"Son, you sound like ya have everythin' all figured out." Jonathan shifted in his seat and had tension in his voice. "I guess we cain't stop ya now that you are an adult. Are ya sure about gold prospectin'? From what we hear, it's not as lucrative as you may think."

"I've gotta try, Pa. I feel it in my bones, an' I'm gonna strike it rich!"

Samuel stood from his seat and walked over to the window and gazed out into the horizon.

At that moment, Mary started to weep. All the emotion of the last year, plus this news, had overwhelmed her.

Upon hearing her whimpers, Samuel knelt besides his mother and held her hand.

"Ma, please don't cry. I won't be far, an' I'll come an' visit."

Mary knew they could not tell him 'no', for it will only cause rebellion and would not help him to progress into manhood and become responsible for himself. She thought of how God allowed the stubborn Israelites to fall to their bad choices, in the hope that they learned from their mistakes and returned to Him realizing they needed His help, guidance, and strength.

She realized her young man had grown into an adult and needed to experience life, make his own decisions, and learn from them. She only hoped Samuel would remember the Bible passages she read to him as a child, as his source of guidance and strength.

After she had calmed herself, she looked deeply into her firstborn's eyes. "Son, ya know we love you very much. We want to support ya in whatever decision ya make. If this is truly the path you feel God is putting in yer heart, then who are we ta stop ya? Is their anythang we can do to help?"

After hearing what his mother had to say, Samuel for the first time realized that he actually did not pray about his decision. Too late now, he thought, for he already had made up his mind to move into the gold country. He returned to his chair and looked intently at his parents.

"I appreciate all you have done fer me, Ma and Pa. Please understand, I've been plannin' this fer so long...this is somethin' I have to do. There are a couple thangs I would like to request. I'm hopin' you will allow me to take Fire an' perhaps one of the shot guns an' revolver."

Concerned for Samuel's welfare Jonathan made an offer. "We can do better than that Sam. Would it help ya out if we gave ya two hundred dollars to start?"

Relieved with his parent's blessings Samuel stood and embraced his parents.

"Thanks, Pa an' Ma. I will repay ya as soon as I strike it rich!"

So Samuel packed his belongings, and the following week he and Fire headed to Jamestown.

13

The Golden Harvest

CHRISTMAS WAS THE ONLY TIME which Samuel would come home and visit for the next four years. His dreams of gold prospecting did not pan out as he had hoped. Penniless and hungry, he ended up working for the Central Pacific Railroad in 1868, only one year after he left home. He worked as a foreman for a Chinese gang of thirty men laying down track through the Sierra Mountain range.

"Come on tie gang...put yer back into it!" Nineteen year old Samuel hollered as he rode his horse, Fire, along the unfinished rails.

The Chinese men removed the ties from the Percheron drawn flatcar and lay them down upon the ballast grade which the Chinese road gang had prepared earlier. After they had finished laying down the ties, the horses pulled the flatcar back to the camp of the rearguard to be reloaded with the steel rails by another Chinese loading gang.

Once loaded, the flatcar would be drawn back to the end

of the track where the next gang unloaded the rails and placed them over the ties.

"Rail gang! Yer turn. Come on men!" Samuel continued to rotate the different Chinese railroad gangs.

Two spikes were distributed per tie along with a rail splice, nuts and bolts to join the following rail.

"Spike gang! Get yer hammers! Come on men!" Samuel yelled.

As the spikes were being driven into each side of the rails, the road gang prepared the next level of ballast up ahead.

"Road gang, take yer shovels men!" Samuel commanded again as he galloped around the railroad laborers, all the while checking the development of their work.

Samuel lived a difficult and dangerous life, especially when it came to blasting tunnels and cliff faces with nitroglycerin. He lost many Chinese men, or "coolies" as they are called, during these blasts. The laborers would be lowered down in baskets along the cliff sides as they placed the explosives into the face of the precipice and discharge it.

In the winter season, the Sierras had so much snow pack that they bore tunnels to travel from the rearguard camp to the work site. Several avalanches had killed groups of workers. Their bodies would not be found until the following spring when the snow melted.

Samuel stayed up nights thinking of these lost men that were not accounted for by the railroad. They buried them in shallow graves nearby the work sites or were left where they fell by a cliff side.

In Samuel's opinion, the Chinese had been much easier to work with than working with the Irish men who grumbled and complained about their monthly wages, and made more demands regarding living comforts than the Chinese men did. Even though the Chinese required certain exotic food delicacies, this did not compare to the Irish men's need for alcohol, women and gambling.

At the Chinese camp, they had few, if not any, rivalries or disputes. There was definitely a sense of community amongst the men. At lunch time, they sat together, bowl in one hand and chop sticks in the other, eating as fast as Westerners would with a fork.

Working with the Chinese men back on the farm gave Samuel a more personal relationship with them than did the other Caucasian railroad workers. Although strict with them, he also had compassion towards them and made certain they received their entire month wage of thirty dollars in change. They tirelessly worked six days a week and had to find accommodation for themselves. They did this by forming communities where they supported each other. The Irish men, however, was given thirty-one dollars a month, including housing.

Samuel found himself drinking heavily and visiting the canvas saloons with the other white railroad men, to keep from falling into depression while at the work camps. The on-going section of track had been followed by a wall tent town whose primary residents are saloon keepers, gamblers, prostitutes, rough men and card sharks. Carnal vices could be fulfilled; whiskey, gambling and the gratifications of the flesh became accustomed staples for the legion of railroad men who flocked to the tents and shacks of this impromptu city. This rugged travelling Sodom and Gomorrah canvas town had been given the name "Hell on Wheels."

The rail workers labored six days a week. Most of them spent their one day off in camp washing clothes, resting, and preparing for the next day. In the evening, the white workers lived licentiously in the canvas saloons. Life was difficult, unbecoming, and lonesome for the men working the rails.

Samuel walked into the twenty feet by twenty feet wall tent filled with gambling tables and thick smoke. Meandering between the gamblers are saloon girls dressed in only their undergarments, corsets and petticoats. Far off to the corner is a crudely made bar attended by a rough-neck bartender.

"Hey Sawyer! Come join us for a game of poker!" Buckeye, another foreman, sat shuffling a deck of cards. He had lost his left eye during a nitroglycerin blast. His replacement eye seemed more like a big brown nut placed in his socket. So Samuel pulled up a chair, and they dealt the cards.

Soon enough, one of the saloon girls came by flaunting herself. "Anythin' I can do for ya gorgeous?" She whispered in Samuel's ear.

"Later Tissa, after my game. In the meantime get me a tall glass of your malt."

After several rounds of drinks and a few hands of poker, Samuel rose from his seat to call it quits. "I'm out."

"Ah come on Coolie lover, don't quit now!" Buckeye growled desiring to recoup his losses.

"Hey, you better watch yer mouth unless ya wanna lose the other eye too!" Samuel snarled back, feeling the whiskey in his system.

Without thinking, Buckeye stood from his chair as the alcohol caused him to lose control and start a brawl.

"Ah you cain't hurt me, Coolie boy!" Buckeye coerced

Samuel. "Come on. Show me watcha got!"

Samuel's blood was boiling. He looked away from Buckeye as if to ignore him, but instead he clenched his right fist and with a sharp turn he slugged Buckeye in his one good eye.

Buckeye tumbled to the ground and shook his head and tried to regain his sight. With blurry vision, he got up and charged at Samuel. Chairs flew, and tables and cards had been tossed around. Eventually, one push led into another, and the whole room was in a brawl. The saloon girls ran out of the tent as bodies came flying out behind them, and the men continued to fight outside. After the fighting had ceased, the bruised and battered railroad men lay in a drunken stupor in the canvas saloon and on the pathways between tents.

"There ya are, gorgeous!" Tissa, the saloon girl, sifted through the bodies passed out on the canvas saloon floor. "Come on. Lean on me. Let me get ya back in my tent, an' I'll have ya feelin' better in no time."

She had found Samuel and helped him up and brought him to her tent where she nursed his wounds and comforted him in the way she knew how. The next morning the men would return to work as if nothing ever happened.

So, Samuel drowned his sorrows with whiskey and a quick hand of poker, and participated in brawls over the Chinese workers as he was ridiculed for his compassion towards them. He often found himself to be seeking the comfort of the arms of a saloon girl who took him for every dime in his pocket.

The Central Pacific Railroad had been finally completed on May 10th, 1869 where it joined rails with the Union

Pacific Railroad at Promontory Summit, Utah. This ended the employment for many of the track layers. Samuel would soon find himself without a job in a couple of years.

SARAH WHO IS NOW SEVENTEEN had finally come out of her mourning after two years. She decided to remove the locket which Joshua had given her, and she tucked it away in a box and hid it in the bottom drawer of her dresser. She blamed God for Joshua's untimely death, and it caused her to become bitter and rebellious.

During the years she mourned, she would finish her chores on the farm and tell her parents she was going to take her horse Belle for a ride. At first, she took refuge at the fort by the creek and spent hours in solitude. But soon that time of reflection turned into resentment towards God for allowing Joshua to die. It came to a point in her life that the anger she suppressed became greater than the love she once had for Joshua.

Two years after his death, she decided to visit Joshua's grave site to say 'goodbye' and finally let go of him. Instead of riding to the fort, she desired to venture in a different direction…into town. This is when she discovered a place called "the Barn" a big building on Fourth Street. During the day, it was transformed into a second-hand store for those wishing to sell used items.

After meandering through the isles, a boldly printed flyer posted on the door caught her attention as she exited the building. *"Contra Dance, Saturday evenings starting at eight o'clock, seventy-five cents admission or one dollar per couple, and all you can eat midnight dinner for fifty cents. Must be twenty-one years or older."* This dance had been advertised in the Merced Herald newspaper and became a favorite meeting place for young people throughout the county.

This spiked Sarah's curiosity. The last two years of mourning seemed to mature Sarah so that she appeared older than her true age of seventeen. She believed she could get away with lying about her age. If anyone inquired about her age, she would tell them that she was born in the year 1847, instead of 1851.

Sarah took the boys bedroom after Samuel left home. She insisted on having her own room because she needed time to be by herself. Naomi and David, who had always been close to one another, did not seem to mind so they shared the same room.

Once everyone had fallen asleep, which was usually by nine o'clock, Sarah tiptoed out of the house, went to the barn to get her horse Belle, and rode into town to attend the contra dance. Afterwards, she would sneak back into the farmhouse and into her room. This happened for some time without anyone in the home noticing.

Sensing Sarah's disconnection, Jonathan and Mary resorted to praying for their daughter and allowing her to go through the grieving process. Whenever they inquired of her condition, she would respond in a curt manner, "I'm fine. Just let me be." So, they stopped asking, but rather reassured her of their love for her.

When Jonathan, Mary, David, and Naomi went to church, Pastor McSwan and Ruth often inquired about Sarah. They continued to tell him that she was not ready to come back or receive anyone yet.

A year later at the Barn, Sarah met a young man named Lad Hampton who was 23 years of age and lived wherever he could lay down his cowboy hat. Most of his time is spent as a cattle gunman out on the range rustling the longhorn belonging to Jackson Montana. On his days off, he frequented the saloons of the hotels closest to the grazing fields. Lately, he had been spending time in the Snelling Hotel and Saloon on the week end, and at the Barn on Saturday evenings, since the cattle had been roaming in nearby Merced Falls.

Lad had been watching Sarah for several weeks now. She was like a magnet to the young men frequenting the Barn because she had a vivacious laugh, a keen sense of humor and wit, and her beauty beckoned attention. Having the option of any man she wanted, she had no fear of hurting any one of their feelings, should they not meet her satisfaction. He examined how she chattered with her lady friends as they compared the gentlemen in the hall, and studied her approach to accept or reject a fellow when they asked her to dance.

"Excuse me Ma'am. May I have this dance?" The gentleman would politely request.

"Why certainly. I would love to!" Sarah extended her gloved hand to his as he led her to the dance floor.

Or, if she decided she did not have any interest in the gentleman, she used her sharp tongue. "Uh, no thank you!"

She would then turn the other way and begin chatting with her friends, leaving the poor fellow standing in disgrace.

Lad thought to himself, "I'm not going to be one of those fellows."

One Saturday evening, he decided to follow Sarah home. He figured she must live nearby since she did not come with a partner or as a couple. It would not be safe for a lady to be riding at night alone if she came from out of town. She rode side saddle as the skirt of her dress and her cape draped to one side of Belle. He followed far enough behind, so that she would not suspect he was following her. After she had passed the school house, she took the wayside path along the wheat field to get back to the farm. From behind the school house, Lad spied as she entered the barn and put her horse away.

Lad returned to the Snelling Hotel where he stayed the night. He would soon find out information about Sarah from the hotel clerk the following Sunday morning.

"Good day, Mr. Hampton. Did you sleep well?" Inquired the clerk.

"Yes, I did as usual." Lad replied as he leaned on the front desk.

"Say, what can you tell me about the beautiful wheat farm on La Grange Road?" Lad pretended to inquire for possible work.

"Oh, that farm belongs to the Sawyer family, Jonathan and Mary, I believe."

"They must have a big family to harvest all that property." Lad stated to provoke an answer.

"Well, I'm told they have four children. I hear their nineteen year old son, Samuel, moved away recently. They have two daughters, Sarah, who is eighteen and Naomi, who is fourteen years old. The youngest son is David, who is, I think, thirteen. It is said that David is growing up to be a real good preacher. He preaches on occasion here in town at the Christian church on Emma Street." The clerk gladly offered the information. "The Sawyers hire the Chinese immigrant workers to do all the farming."

This was enough gossip for Lad. "So Sarah is only eighteen," he thought to himself.

"Well the farm is, without a doubt, beautiful. Okay. I better be on my way ta work. Thank you again for yer hospitality!" Lad said as he paid his room bill and walked out of the hotel and rode off on his grey horse back to Merced Falls.

The following Saturday night at the Barn, Lad stood by the bar sipping on a malt and kept a watchful eye for Sarah. She appeared around her usual time of 9:45 in the evening.

Removing her riding cape and hood drew the eyes of every gentleman in the room as she wore a ruffled red and black gown which revealed her soft shoulders and neck. This is a dress that Sarah had made after purchasing material in town. Her hair is parted in the center as silky brown ringlets, pulled to the back of her head, flowed down upon her shoulders.

She looked around the hall to find her lady friends and sat next to them. He watched as she accepted dances, or shamed some poor chap, and sipped on a glass of wine joyfully laughing.

Lad disclosed his plans to the waiter.

"I would like to pay for the drinks for the lady in red. Why don't you send her another glass of whatever she is drinking and let her know it came from me and that her tab is paid for, all right partner?" Lad handed him a healthy tip.

"Yes, Sir. I'll take care of it immediately. Shall I give her your name?"

"Nope, just point me out."

"Okay."

The waiter poured Sarah a goblet of wine and delivered it to her.

"Ma'am. This is from the gentleman sitting by the bar. He says he will cover your tab for the night." He handed Sarah the glass and pointed to Lad whose back was faced towards her.

"Oh how gracious of him. Please give him my gratitude," Sarah told the waiter who sent the message to Lad.

Upon hearing this, Lad simply turned and tipped his hat to Sarah who peered at him from across the room.

For several Saturday nights Lad paid for Sarah's drinks, but never requested to dance with her. This annoyed Sarah and her curiosity could no longer hold her down.

"Who is this mysterious man and why hasn't he asked me to dance?" she thought.

Lad wore a black coachman hat, dressed in a dark brushed twill longhorn shirt, brown Cassidy canvas trousers, leather Duke Vest, and Pale Rider boots. Hanging low on the side of his hips is his gun belt and colt revolvers. By the evening time, his face had the cast of a five o'clock shadow that added to his rugged features. Lad's strategy is to lure Sarah over to him and not the other way around. He continued to purchase her drinks never asking her to dance.

His tactic worked because Sarah felt obligated to at least show appreciation to this man who had been paying her way. So, she finally found the courage to walk up to Lad and thank him in her haughty manner. Lad could sense her walking towards him and so he faced the bar and took a big gulp of his malt.

Sarah tapped his left shoulder, and he turned to hear a barrage of words coming from her sweet lips.

"Sir, I've been meaning to thank ya personally fer yer generosity for the last few Saturday evenings. Please sir, ya need to stop as I sense an obligation ta somehow repay ya."

"Yes Ma'am, as ya wish." Lad replied in a low, raspy tone. He didn't show any sign of emotion, and turned his back to her, put his money down on the counter, and walked out the door. He left Sarah standing there looking like the fool.

This infuriated Sarah. "Who does this man think he is?!" she thought to herself as she stood justly embarrassed. This had never happened to her before. She sensed everyone staring at her.

So she turned on her heels and immediately followed Lad outside screaming.

"Look here! Who do ya think ya are treating me this way?!" as she grabbed hold of his arm to turn him around to face her.

"What way are ya referring to Ma'am? For being a gentleman and buying your drinks or being a gentleman and doing what you asked of me?" He retorted with a sharp tongue as his eyes pierced hers.

Sarah's jaw dropped as she had been dealt her own game. She was getting ready to slap Lad, but he grasped her hand and drew her into his arms and kissed her. At first she resisted, but all emotions told her to let go as she swooned into his embrace.

"Now...can we start over?" Lad gazed deep into her softened eyes. "My name is Lad Hampton, and I had no intentions of you repaying me."

"I...I...I'm Sarah." She tried to get hold of herself and find strength in her knees to stand on her own. This sensation had not come upon her since the time she kissed Joshua at the fort by the creek.

"I know Sarah Sawyer. Now how 'bout we take a seat out here in the moonlight and get acquainted with one another?" Lad loosened his arms and held the small of her back, directing her to the steps leading to the Barn.

This would be the beginning of an emotionally steeped relationship for Sarah and Lad. They ended up getting married six months later by a judge in Mariposa County and living in a small cabin in the cedar groves.

NAOMI TURNED FOURTEEN when Sarah and Lad eloped in the summer of 1869. Her once head strong propensity became a blessing rather than a curse when pointed in the right direction. After the lesson she learned with the Edgar children, and watching her eldest brother and sister struggle in their lives, she hoped to learn from their mistakes and reconstruct her own life.

She never did hear from the Edgars after they were expelled from school. It is said that the whole family moved to Merced Falls closer to the lumber mill where their father worked. She looked back and realized how tender a root she had been in the Lord and that she lacked the discernment to know evil from good.

Naomi excelled in school and finished early by one year with outstanding grades. Mr. Cavern had seen the remarkable difference in Naomi's attitude when she returned. Being grounded caused her to appreciate the ability of having the freedom to choose and that she should not take it for granted, for the wrong decision could put her back into bondage to appropriate consequences. So, Naomi strived to keep her liberties by allowing God to direct her heart and mind to make proper choices.

She had taken over the responsibilities which Sarah once had tending to the animals and helping Mary out in the farmhouse. She took the front bedroom and David the back. Naomi loved her parents and living on the farm, and they appreciated her efforts. To find direction for her life and help support the McSwan family, she returned to church not too long after Joshua's death.

Naomi enjoyed riding the horses Jack and Belle, and herding the oxen and cattle. She also found pleasure in doing the practical work around the farm and plowing the fields with her father.

"Naomi, why don't you drive the wagon this mornin' ta church?" Jonathan suggested. "It's time ya start takin' the reins."

"Really, Pa…can I?" Naomi asked with enthusiasm.

"Yep, ya sure can! In fact, I'd like to start training ya to drive the team. Now that Samuel and Sarah are gone, I could use another driver to haul the wheat to the flour mill in Merced Falls."

Both Mary and Jonathan were amazed at Naomi's rate of maturity, and how responsible she had become. They became pleased with Naomi's development in her character, especially after the ordeal with the Edgar children.

Her appreciation for life had been exemplified in her behavior and work. One afternoon following the church service in the late spring of 1869, she chose to reconcile her relationship with Mr. Jacobi.

"Hello Mr. Jacobi. Do you remember me?" Naomi probed his memory since he had not seen her for three years.

He examined Naomi's face through his spectacles. She was six inches taller from the time he had last met her at the Snelling Courthouse.

"No. It can't be. Naomi?"

"Yes Sir. That's me!"

"My! You've grown!" Mr. Jacobi cheerfully laughed out loud.

"Yes, in more ways than one! I was just a silly little girl, with silly little notions way back when. I've learned my lesson since I last saw you and I want ta apologize to you again for the trouble I caused you…stealin' an' all. Is there anythin' I can do to repay you for the bad thangs I did? Will ya forgive me?"

"Oh Naomi, dat is vater under za bridge. I forgave you a long time ago. Besides, as you said, you vere a child back zen. Ve all made silly mistakes like dat before. Even I stole from a store ven I vas a little boy. In my days, Papa gave us da rod ven ve vere punished." Mr. Jacobi laughed as he pointed to his buttock.

"Papa made me break my piggybank and pay da owner myself. I learned my lesson. Maybe dat is vhy I decided to have my own store to prove I can be an honest merchant as vell as be an honest customer."

"Well, Mr. Jacobi, I would like to do this for ya too. That is if ya could use some help and if ya can learn to trust me. I'd love to work fer ya an' work real hard to prove that I can be honest." She did her best to convince him.

Thinking as he crossed his arms in front of his chest, Mr. Jacobi observed Naomi for a while. He slowly paced back and forth behind the counter rubbing his chin with his index finger, looking at the floor, then at the ceiling as he tried to figure out the working schedule, and how he might employ her. He had always wanted more counter support while he managed the register or as he stocked the merchandise. "Yes, this would work," he thought.

"Ya. I sink I could use your help behind za counter. Vhen are you available?"

Naomi responded with a big smile. "I can work in the afternoons for you and start right away!"

"Okay. How does Tuesday through Saturday from one to five o'clock verk for you?" Mr. Jacobi suggested. "It vill be part time for now."

"This is perfect!"

"Okay. Zen we have an agreement. Ya?" He extended his hand to shake hers.

"We have an agreement." Naomi shook his hand. So Naomi started the following week and continued to work for him in 1871 when David began preaching.

DAVID IS NOW FIFTEEN YEARS OLD and preaches occasionally for Pastor McSwan at the new church in Snelling on Emma and Fourth Street. From the time of Joshua's death, Pastor McSwan discontinued the camp meetings. He did not have the heart to take any risks of illnesses to his family again, and put them through the remembrance of that fateful night.

So Pastor McSwan concentrated on holding church services in the town. He poured himself into teaching David the Scriptures and had him fill the pulpit too. He had plans of allowing David to preach full time once he turned sixteen years old, and had finished school.

In 1872, after turning sixteen, David began his sermon in the book of James 1:2-6, *"My brethren, count it all joy when you fall into various trials, knowing that the testing of your faith produces patience. But let patience have its perfect work, that you may be perfect and complete, lacking nothing. If any of you lacks wisdom, let him ask of God, who gives to all liberally and without reproach, and it will be given to him. But let him ask in faith, with no doubting, for he who doubts is like a wave of the sea driven and tossed by the wind."* David read and then gave an illustration.

"For years now I watched as my parents struggled through so many trials an' tribulations in their lives. My father had been wounded during the Civil War which nearly took his life, an' our farm in Kentucky was ravaged by this terrible battle. Shortly after, was the six month arduous move to California, followed by starting a new life of farming in Snelling. In addition, they had troubles with the four of us siblings growin' up. Most difficult of all is the loss of the ones dearest to them, either by death or by unforeseen circumstances. These moments of travail an' heartache can test an' shake any man or woman's faith. I continue to observe them, an' how they patiently persevered through these situations, never losing faith in God to have victory over their lives an' the lives of their children." David gave the illustration with his father and mother as the example.

"Their faith in an almighty an' all-knowing God, has given them the strength, patience, hope, an' peace needed to endure these moments. God always provided a lesson for one of us to learn through these trials an' tribulations. Thus, my parents never feared, but rather had peace an' joy knowin' God uses all things for good to those who love Him." David explained passionately.

"This is the attitude an' perspective which you, who are in Christ Jesus, should have an' hope for. God shapes you an' makes you more like His Son through the difficulties you encounter in your life. Throughout these circumstances, He may be teachin' you about love, patience, joy an' peace, kindness, gentleness, goodness, faithfulness, an' self-control. It tests your faith to see if you truly believe upon the promises in His Word through your obedience to abide to His commands. As you experience His faithfulness to fulfill his spiritual principles, your understandin' grows deeper, an' your faith becomes stronger, an' the trials become much easier to bear. In place of anxiety is joy an' peace, with understandin' that the testin' has a purpose an' plan for sanctification in your life. So, be patient having peace an' joy in knowing that God will be faithful to His promises! Amen!" David concluded the sermon.

Jonathan and Mary had tears well up in their eyes realizing their youngest of the family discerned the struggles they had gone through in the last ten years. They were so thankful for God who was faithful to work in the life of David and continues to work in the lives of Samuel, Sarah, and Naomi.

EARLY ONE SATURDAY MORNING after the golden wheat had been harvested, Jonathan and Mary leaned back in their wingback chairs in his office. The crops had been hearty and prosperous. They sipped on their hot cup of coffee as they looked at the pictures of their children on the fireplace mantel. Tears came to their eyes as they both reminisced and discussed the good and difficult times their family had experienced within the last ten years.

At that moment, Jonathan remembered a particular event and its connection to their lives. "Honey, do you remember the first church service we attended with Pastor McSwan?"

"Hum...let me think." Mary tilted her head back against the chair. "Yes, I do, Dear. We met in the Snelling courthouse."

"Do ya remember what Pastor McSwan preached about?" Jonathan asked inquisitively aiming to make a point.

"Sort of," Mary thought deeply. "I think he spoke about the Parable of the Sower."

"You're correct! Do ya remember the message?" Jonathan continued to probe her mind.

"I believe he used the analogy of the sower who planted seeds in different types of ground. The seeds, which fell on the wayside, had been eatin' up by birds. The seeds, which fell on stony places, grew fast, but also died quickly because of the sun's scorching, and not having enough soil to root themselves. Some of the seeds fell amongst thorns and had been choked out. But some of the seeds fell on good soil and yielded a crop of one hundred fold, some sixty, and some thirty." Mary recited the Parable of the Sower. "Why do ya ask Jonathan?"

"Well, I realized that God was using this parable to prepare us for what we would be experiencing the following seven years of our lives with our children at that time!" Jonathan beamed with resolution.

"Ya see, the Word of God is the seed that is planted in a Believer's heart. The seed, or Word, had been planted in Samuel's wayward heart, but the cares of the world, 'gold prospectin', took hold of him and pulled him away from the Lord." Intrigued with Jonathan's analogy, Mary sat at the edge of her chair.

"Then the Word was planted in Sarah's stony heart. I believe she loved the Lord fer the wrong reasons. She really was in love with Joshua, the Pastor's son. So, she had no depth or rich enough soil in her heart to grow in God's Word. When the trial of Joshua's death came upon her, she did not have root or comfort in God's Word, so she strayed away in her belief in the Lord," Jonathan continued.

"Simultaneously, the Word had been planted in Naomi's heart, but she had been choked out by the thorns, the Edgar children and their bad behavior. So she never gained any depth in her faith in God. I thank God that He gave us wisdom to provide the correct discipline, and now she is back on the right track with God!" Then Jonathan took a deep sigh of relief.

"However, the Word of God had been planted in David's heart full of rich love for the Lord. Now he has a wonderful relationship with Jesus and is developing into an outstanding preacher being used of God!" Jonathan smiled contentedly.

"Ya see, my Dear, God wanted to show us what the golden harvest would be in our lives. We are the sowers…the Sawyers!" Jonathan chuckled at his pun. "I'm gonna continue to trust Him for the complete salvation of our children because he still has many parables to apply to their lives." Jonathan laughed with confidence in his heart.

This word of wisdom brought both Jonathan and Mary much comfort, peace, and hope for their children, knowing that God's Word does not return void. They planted the seed in their hearts and someone else will have to water it. Lifting their family up in prayer, they continued to look to God for His guidance and His care. They had comfort knowing that God had a plan for each of their children in His golden harvest.

ABOUT THE AUTHOR

ROSANNA CEREZO SHARPS is a Pastor's wife who loves God's children of all ages and exudes compassion for the struggles they face daily in their lives. Realizing *there is nothing new under the sun**, she continues to discover the ability to overcome many of life's trials through the application of God's Word.

Sometimes when vicariously experiencing someone else's struggles as they strive to maintain their course on the *narrow path*, it can help one to understand their own sense of direction. With this in mind, the author prayerfully crafted Golden Harvest, a historic fictional story that wraps itself with warmth and affection around the parables in the Bible to help enlighten the pathway of God's people.

Rosanna studied Psychology at Southwestern College, and theology at Calvary Chapel Bible College. At the present, she teaches Bible studies for women, youth, and grade school children at the church where her husband pastors in Rio Vista, California. They have one musically gifted son whom she home schooled from first grade through high school. Her passion is studying God's Word, praying, loving her family, having fellowship with other Believers, singing worship songs, and traveling to places and enjoying God's creation. When there is spare time, she enjoys settling into a cozy chair and crocheting or knitting.

* Ecclesiastes 1:9

The Parable of the Sower

Matthew 13:1-23 (KJV)

13:1 The same day went Jesus out of the house, and sat by the sea side. 2 And great multitudes were gathered together unto him, so that he went into a ship, and sat; and the whole multitude stood on the shore.

3 And he spake many things unto them in parables, saying, Behold, a sower went forth to sow; 4 And when he sowed, some seeds fell by the way side, and the fowls came and devoured them up: 5 Some fell upon stony places, where they had not much earth: and forthwith they sprung up, because they had no deepness of earth: 6 And when the sun was up, they were scorched; and because they had no root, they withered away. 7 And some fell among thorns; and the thorns sprung up, and choked them: 8 But other fell into good ground, and brought forth fruit, some an hundredfold, some sixtyfold, some thirtyfold. 9 Who hath ears to hear, let him hear.

10 And the disciples came, and said unto him, Why speakest thou unto them in parables?

11 He answered and said unto them, Because it is given unto you to know the mysteries of the kingdom of heaven, but to them it is not given. 12 For whosoever hath, to him shall be given, and he shall have more abundance: but whosoever hath not, from him shall be taken away even that he hath. 13 Therefore speak I to them in parables: because they seeing see not; and hearing they hear not, neither do they understand. 14 And in them is fulfilled the

prophecy of Esaias, which saith, By hearing ye shall hear, and shall not understand; and seeing ye shall see, and shall not perceive: 15 For this people's heart is waxed gross, and their ears are dull of hearing, and their eyes they have closed; lest at any time they should see with their eyes, and hear with their ears, and should understand with their heart, and should be converted, and I should heal them.

16 But blessed are your eyes, for they see: and your ears, for they hear. 17 For verily I say unto you, That many prophets and righteous men have desired to see those things which ye see, and have not seen them; and to hear those things which ye hear, and have not heard them.

18 Hear ye therefore the parable of the sower. 19 When any one heareth the word of the kingdom, and understandeth it not, then cometh the wicked one, and catcheth away that which was sown in his heart. This is he which received seed by the way side. 20 But he that received the seed into stony places, the same is he that heareth the word, and anon with joy receiveth it; 21 Yet hath he not root in himself, but dureth for a while: for when tribulation or persecution ariseth because of the word, by and by he is offended. 22 He also that received seed among the thorns is he that heareth the word; and the care of this world, and the deceitfulness of riches, choke the word, and he becometh unfruitful. 23 But he that received seed into the good ground is he that heareth the word, and understandeth it; which also beareth fruit, and bringeth forth, some an hundredfold, some sixty, some thirty.

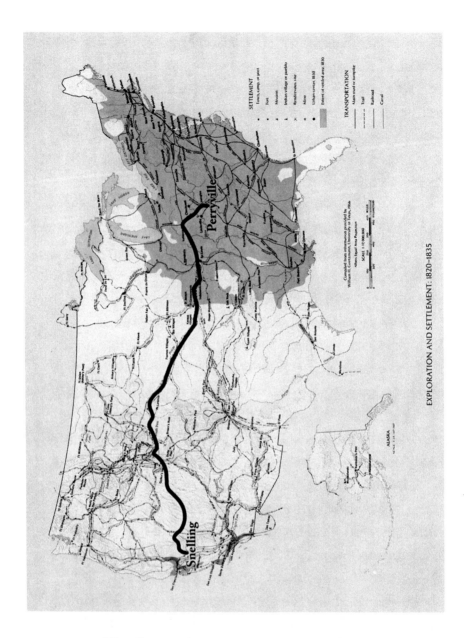

The Sawyer's wagon train route from
Perryville, Kentucky to Snelling, California.

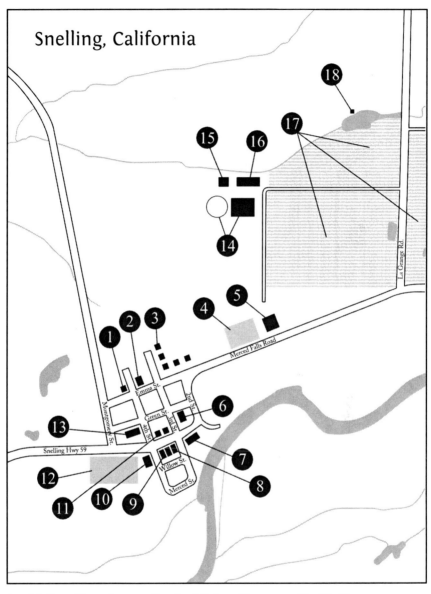

Snelling, California

1. McSwan Home *	7. Jacobi's Store **	13. The Barn
2. Church	8. Snelling Saloon	14. Sawyer Barn *
3. Edgar House *	9. Meat Market	15. Sawyer Cabin *
4. Cemetery	10. Livery Stable	16. Sawyer Farmhouse *
5. Snelling School	11. Dr. Cassidy's Clinic *	17. Sawyer Wheat Field *
6. County Courthouse	12. Chinese Camp	18. Sawyer Tree Fort *

Fictitious location ** *Fictitious name*

ABOVE: Snelling Courthouse, built in 1857.

OPPOSITE TOP: The Jacob's Store, built in 1858.
OPPOSITE BOTTOM: Methodist Church, built in 1871.

IOOF Dance Hall (a.k.a. The Barn).

CPSIA information can be obtained at www.ICGtesting.com
262153BV00003B/3/P

9 780983 447405